WHEN WE FALL

SHIRLEY SIATON

WHEN WE FALL
Two Love Stories

Originally published as 'Angel' (August 2023) and 'The Last Divide' (November 2023).

Copyright © 2024 Shirley Siaton Parabia

ALL RIGHTS RESERVED.
No part of this book may be reproduced or used in any manner without the prior written permission of the copyright owner, except for the use of brief quotations in a book review. To request permission, contact the publisher at books@inkysword.com.

This is a work of fiction. Names, characters, businesses, events, and incidents are the products of the author's imagination. Any resemblance to actual persons, living or dead, or actual events is purely coincidental.

All brand and product names used in this book are trademarks, registered trademarks, or trade names of their respective owners. Inky Sword Book Publishing is not associated with any product or vendor in this book.

ISBN 978-6-21-490056-5

First Edition, January 2024

Published by Shirley S. Parabia
Cover design by Artscandare
Interior formatting by Champagne Book Design

Inky Sword Book Publishing
Barangay Quezon, Arevalo, Iloilo City 5000
Republic of the Philippines
inkysword.com

CONTENT WARNINGS

Warnings for explicit content, mild profanity, and references to violence and death

Recommended for mature readers 18 years old and above.

To all my readers

With all my love

CONTENTS

Content Warnings   iii
Foreword   ix

The Last Divide   xiii

Prologue   1
Drawn

One   9
Reverie

Two   17
Return

Three   25
Rewind

Four   37
Resurface

Five   47
Restart

Six   55
Recall

Seven   65
Remnant

Eight   79
Revelation

Nine   97
Resonance

Ten   109
Restraint

Eleven *Recompense*	119
Twelve *Remainder*	127
Thirteen *Retrace*	143
Fourteen *Restitution*	155
Epilogue *Crossed*	167
Angel	175
One *Stranger*	179
Two *Criminal*	187
Three *Farewell*	201
Four *Reckoning*	209
Five *Prison*	217
Six *Storm*	225
About The Author	231
Links	233

FOREWORD

The previous year, 2023, was the time I officially became a book author. When my first poetry collection was published last February, never in my wildest dreams have I ever imagined my stories and poems would reach so many people by the time the year ended.

For the ten and a half months of my first calendar year in publication, two of my books stood out from the rest: *Angel* and *The Last Divide*. Both are fairly quick romance reads; each is a novella about a Filipino couple in my hometown, Iloilo City. No two love stories could be more different, though: one is a gritty tale of a crime family enforcer and a college girl; the other of two overachievers driven by a love so strong neither time nor distance could dull their passion.

At the heart of it all, however, is the kind of love that weathers storms—the kind of love that blooms and endures even when the most merciless of rains fall.

Through these stories, I wish to share this kind of epic, timeless love with you.

WHEN WE FALL

TWO LOVE STORIES

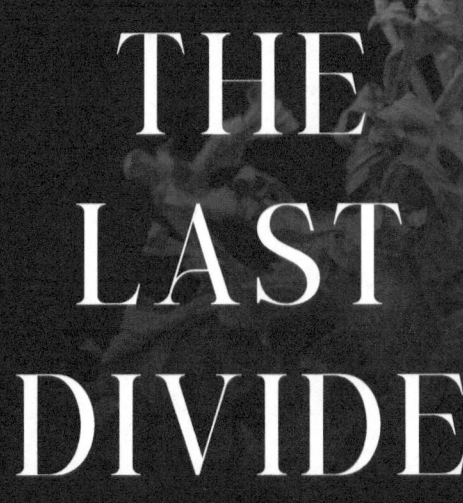

THE
LAST
DIVIDE

PLAYLIST

"Indestructible"
Alisha's Attic

"Konstantine"
Something Corporate

"What If"
Kate Winslet

"Someday"
Nickelback

"Moments Like This"
Allison Krauss

"Stay"
Hurts

"Baby Can I Hold You"
Tracy Chapman

PROLOGUE

Royce

DRAWN

Why was he nervous?

School was over.

There were no more grades to reach and work hard for, no more competitive quiz bees, no more sports tournaments.

Royce Duran knew he should feel relieved.

Relief was the last word he'd use to describe what he felt at the moment. His pulse was racing; he was dizzy, and his throat felt closed and dry.

She was late.

In the late afternoon light, the football field before him looked desolate and abandoned. The grass had grown a little too high and unruly; the ground was still muddy and partially upturned from the typhoon the week before.

He glanced at his watch, shifting slightly in his seat on the empty bleachers. She was usually punctual. Just as he began to feel agitated, he caught sight of her approaching figure.

Koreen Cisco was smaller than him by nearly a foot, barely reaching five feet tall. Her long, straight black hair swayed with each step. Even across the distance between them, her cat-like eyes bored into him like sniper rifles.

"Hey," she called out as she approached, her voice betraying a hint of the awkwardness that hung between them.

They were used to competing side by side and pushing each other to excel, but they rarely spoke privately or found themselves alone together.

"Hey, Koreen. Thanks for coming. Would you like to sit down?"

One of her dark brows shot into her hairline, an expression he associated with her uncertainty. She usually looked at him that way whenever he uttered an answer to a problem in Math class. Most, if not all, of the time, she would get the correct answer.

She settled on the same level of the bleachers, about two feet away from where he sat. She crossed her arms and regarded him with the same piercing, doubting look.

"This is weird, Duran. I thought you were screwing with me when you said you wanted to meet."

"Wouldn't dream of it," he replied with a smile, attempting to lighten the mood.

"Don't think I'm here to do you any favors. It's more curiosity than anything else." She wrinkled her nose at him. "Be honest, then, what's this about? Something important?"

Her bluntness was one of the things he secretly appreciated about her.

"Not really," he replied with a shrug. "I just wanted to say goodbye."

"Goodbye? You're leaving?"

"Yep." He watched her reaction closely. "My family's leaving town."

"Why? Where are you going?" she muttered, her eyes downcast. "I thought you're staying in Iloilo. Get into law school and all that."

He nodded. "That was the plan. But things change. With the bank closing last year, it's been hard on my parents. My father found a new job in Manila. As for me, I was lucky enough my state university scholarship allowed me to pick any campus with an available spot."

"Wow," she replied. "Congratulations. Manila, huh?"

"Looks like it."

They were both silent for a while, watching the sun set over the muddy field.

She was the first to speak. "Well, I'm staying right here, getting my teaching degree."

"Being a teacher has always suited you," he said honestly, giving her a sidelong glance. "I've learned a lot from you, you know."

"Likewise," she replied, a small smile tugging at her lips.

"You know the best part about this? There'll be one less person around to annoy you."

She chuckled. "You're right. Things will be different without you."

"Yeah. Whichever way you look at it, we won't be around to annoy each other anymore."

They shared a light laugh, but, as the words left his lips, Royce felt a chill in the air that had nothing to do with the recent heavy rains. Their fierce competition over the years had created a strange yet undeniable bond. Separation was something new.

He took a deep breath and stood up with his hands in his pockets, feeling as though the fading light of day mirrored the closing chapter of his life in this city. He turned to look at the girl next to him, her glistening black hair catching the last rays of sunlight.

His greatest rival at school since first grade. His training partner in Karate since they were both six. They had shared valedictory honors in elementary and high school. They had both won regional kata championships in the past year.

She was practically part of him, wasn't she?

"Koreen," he began, hesitating for a moment before continuing. "I just wanted to say…I'm sorry for being such a pain in your ass since we were little."

"You're a good kind of pain, Duran—the kind that keeps me on my toes." She stood up and, to his surprise, moved closer to him. "Thanks for always pushing me a little bit more."

"You did the same for me," he admitted, acutely aware of the increasing tightness in his throat as he looked into her eyes.

Looking away, he unzipped his backpack and retrieved a small bundle wrapped in cloth. From the canvas bag, he pulled out his black belt in Karate, its fabric worn from years of use.

"I want you to have this," he said, holding it out to her.

"With the way we've trained together over the years, our belts belong together, too."

She hesitated, her eyes flicking between the belt and his face. "This belt's yours. Why wouldn't you practice Karate anymore?"

"Maybe I will, but I'll have to start over at another club. If I do find a new one, I doubt it will be the same as the one we've got. I'd rather my belt stay with a champion, at my home dojo."

She looked at him closely for a while, her eyes thoughtful.

"Fine." Koreen relented after a moment, albeit reluctantly. "I'll hold on to it. For now. You can have it back anytime, okay?"

"Thanks." He nodded and put the belt back in its case before handing it to her. Their hands brushed against each other for a fleeting moment, sending a jolt of electricity up his arm. They both pulled away quickly, as if burned by the contact.

There had always been a barrier between them, something that the years and their fierce rivalry had put up between them. It was an invisible wall that stopped them from crossing into unknown territory, and now it seemed more impenetrable than ever.

"Is that all you wanted?" Koreen clutched the case of his belt tightly, her fingers tracing the embroidered letters of his name on the silken cloth.

Royce hesitated. "Yeah...actually, no." He reached into his bag once more and pulled out a black box containing a single white anemone, its petals lined with thin yellow, pink, and red stripes.

"This is for you." He held the box out with both hands.

Her eyes widened in surprise. "What's this?"

"It's an anemone," he replied, trying to sound casual despite the pounding of his heart.

"Aren't these supposed to be rare? And expensive, too…" Her voice trailed off as she looked at him and the box doubtfully.

He swallowed the lump in his throat, struggling to find the words to explain the significance of the anemone.

But the words never came, eclipsed by nerves and fear.

"Can you do me a favor and just take it?" he finally asked, his voice strained. "Don't you like it?"

"I like it very much." Her eyes never left the flower as she answered his question quietly and quickly. She reached out, her fingers brushing against the box before she took it from him. "Thanks."

"You're welcome."

Koreen held the box to her chest as if it were something fragile, not meeting his eyes as she spoke. "Does Kenneth know you're leaving?"

Her younger brother was one his closest friends, a basketball buddy since childhood. "He doesn't yet. I'll tell him and the others about the move during the game tonight. You're the first to know."

Her gaze moved to his face this time, making him feel very self-conscious. "I guess this is it."

He took a deep breath, feeling his head spin as he did. "Right. Just…take care of yourself, okay? And keep in touch. Let me know if you do decide to compete in the nationals."

She nodded. "Take care of yourself, Duran. Good luck with everything."

He dared to look into her eyes as he gave her an awkward gesture that seemed a cross between a wave and a salute. "Goodbye, Koreen."

Koreen seemed to want to say something more, but instead, she turned and walked away.

As he watched her retreating back, Royce desperately wanted to call out her name. He wasn't sure why, but he would have given anything to make her stop and at least look at him over her shoulder, for perhaps the final time.

Instead, he could only stare at the space she had gone into, long after she was out of sight.

ONE

Koreen

REVERIE

SHE STOOD IN FRONT OF THE CLASSROOM AS SHE collected the last of the answer sheets, nodding appreciatively as her students stood in a quiet queue.

In life and in the classroom, Koreen Cisco prided herself on maintaining order and discipline. Today was no exception, as the weekly quiz in her Modern Algebra class wrapped up like clockwork.

"Thank you, everyone," she said as the final paper was handed to her. "I'll have these graded by Monday. Have a great weekend."

The final bell of the school week tolled. Murmuring amongst themselves, her students filed out of the room, leaving her alone to gather her belongings and prepare for the next part of her day.

Her life was a whirlwind of activity. In addition to teaching, she also worked part-time as a Karate instructor at her old martial arts gym and as a trainer for a local BPO training center.

Growing up, Koreen had always been fiercely competitive and dedicated, excelling in both academics and sports. Her father, a math teacher himself, had passed away when she was in her first year of college, leaving her with the responsibility of helping her mother and younger brother. Through hard work and determination, she and her mother, who worked as an accountant for the city government, had managed to put her brother through medical school.

Even now, with her mother retired and Kenneth working as a doctor on a residency in another province, she continued to push herself in every aspect of her life. Her days were long and demanding, but she wouldn't have it any other way.

She knew no other way.

As she shouldered her bag and locked her classroom door, her phone rang. It was her brother calling.

"Hey, Ken. How's the residency going?"

"Busy, as always," he replied with a tired chuckle. "But it's good. I'm learning a lot, especially techniques on how to stay awake for seventy-two hours straight. How about you? How are things?"

"Same as always. Teaching, Karate, training…the usual."

"Always on the go, huh?"

She bristled slightly at his loaded comment, aware of the defensive edge in her own voice. "I enjoy it. Keeps me sharp."

"Yeah, but just make sure you're taking care of yourself

too, okay?" His voice turned gentle, almost placating. She wondered if they taught this kind of thing at medical school: how to deal with stubborn patients—or older sisters. "Mama called me the other day and told me she's worried you don't seem to be slowing down at all."

"Slowing down?" she scoffed. "What for? Life doesn't stop just because we're tired."

"Well, she said you were working even when you were sick last time. You can't keep pushing yourself like that, Koreen. Your body might give up on you."

She rolled her eyes at his comment. "Ken, it was just a seasonal cold. Nothing to worry about."

"Still, you need to take better care of your health. Make sure you're eating well, getting enough sleep, and maybe consider taking a break every now and then. It wouldn't hurt."

"Alright, alright," she conceded, not wanting to prolong the conversation. "I'll try to take it easy. Thanks for looking out for me."

"Of course," he said, before pausing for a moment. "Oh, by the way, have you heard from Royce lately?"

"Royce who?" She waved goodbye to a small group of teachers exiting the faculty room. The day had ended for the people at school, but she was barely halfway done with hers.

"Royce Duran," Kenneth clarified.

The name stopped her train of thought.

Royce.

Memories of their fierce academic rivalry and intense kata training sessions came flooding back. He'd been part of her life for years, ever since they were four.

She still thought of him, after all these years, whenever she demonstrated the Pinan sequences. No one could ever quite match his power in kata. She had the technique down pat, but sheer passion in every single move…Royce had that, and more.

"Uh, no," she managed to say, shaking off her reverie. "I haven't heard much from him since we graduated high school. Why?"

"He's visiting Iloilo for a business project or something. He reached out to me and told me he wanted to catch up while he's here. I'll see if I can get some of the old gang back together on a weekend to shoot some hoops."

Despite herself, her curiosity was piqued. "I've seen some of his posts online, but we haven't messaged each other or anything. He's still working in Saudi, isn't he?"

After finishing college in Manila, she knew that Royce had taken a job in Saudi Arabia. He had never come back to Iloilo City since he'd told her his family was moving.

"Yeah, he was still in Saudi when he messaged me, but he was getting ready to travel here. Maybe you'll run into him while he's in town."

"Maybe," she echoed uncertainly. After nearly fifteen years, seeing him again—in person—seemed a strange, distant possibility. He was only ever a face from her past, captured in old photographs.

"Anyway, I should get back to work," said Kenneth. "Take care of yourself, sis. And if you do see Royce, let me know how it goes."

"Sure thing. Take care, too."

As they said their goodbyes and hung up, Koreen couldn't help but feel a strange mix of emotions. She appreciated her brother's concern, but part of her bristled at the thought of someone telling her to slow down. She couldn't deny that she was overworked, but hadn't she been managing just fine all these years?

Her ultimate dream was to open her own BPO training center, a place where she could teach people the tools and tricks of the industry that had helped keep her family afloat since she was in college. She'd worked part-time as a call center agent and a medical transcriptionist while completing her Education degree.

Her dream business seemed more and more distant with each passing day, despite her tireless efforts. Raising funds was her greatest challenge; everything got more and more expensive as time went on, while her net income barely inched upward.

And then there was Royce—the boy who had once pushed her to her limits, both mentally and physically. What would it be like to see him again, after so many years?

He's a man now, she corrected herself. High school was a lifetime ago.

But his black belt was still with her, safely kept next to her Karate trophies in their place of honor, on a living room display shelf at her parent's home.

Lost in thought as she made her way to the parking area of the high school, Koreen barely noticed her phone vibrating in her hand again.

Glancing at the screen, she saw that it was from the gym. She swiped to pick up the call.

"Hey, Maggie."

"Hi, Koreen, I'm so sorry to bother you. I hope I'm not interrupting your class or anything." The receptionist's tone was both apologetic and urgent.

"No, it's fine. I'm done at school. I was just on my way to the training center. What's up?"

"Something important. We have a high-profile client who specifically requested a one-on-one session with you."

"Really?" Koreen was intrigued by the sudden request. She was no stranger to special sessions, but this came out of the blue. She usually saw these logged in her schedule at the gym weeks in advance. "I don't mind, but shouldn't I assess their skills first before accepting so I can prepare?"

"No need for that," Maggie replied, a little too cheerfully. "You know the client quite well, actually. It's Royce Duran. Leo told me you used to train with him."

Koreen's heart skipped a beat, and her grip tightened around the phone.

It had to be him, of course. After years of silence, it was typical of Royce Duran to simply reappear and weave his way back into her life, as if he'd never left.

She sighed, hoping Maggie wouldn't pick up her exasperation through the line. "When is it scheduled for?"

"Tomorrow, at four."

Saturday was her busiest in terms of teaching Karate. Starting at one in the afternoon, she had a kids' class, a thirty-minute kata technique session with some athletes competing at a local tournament, and an advanced class for brown belts and higher. Four o'clock was smack dab in between the last two, but she could manage it. She could do with the extra money.

"Fine. Book the session."

"Great," came the receptionist's enthusiastic response. "I'll see you tomorrow, Koreen."

"See you, Maggie. Thanks."

As she hung up and quickly made her way to her trusty red Corolla, her mind raced with thoughts about Royce, their history, and what his return meant for her and her hectic, carefully constructed world.

If it meant anything at all.

But there was no time to dwell on that now; Koreen had work to do. Her class with beginner transcriptionists was due to start in an hour.

She squared her shoulders, got into the car, and drove off, trying to ignore the pounding of her heart.

TWO

Royce

RETURN

SUCCESS WAITED FOR NO ONE; NEITHER DID THE CITY before him.

Royce Duran stood by the window of his hotel suite overlooking the bustling streets of Iloilo. The cityscape stretched out before him, glistening in the late afternoon sun. It had rained on and off since he arrived three days ago, but, today, the clear skies were a welcome sight.

So much had changed in the past fifteen years in his hometown. Where before there were empty fields in the outskirts of the city, imposing buildings with modern architecture now stood in their place. These new buildings had become the hub for telecommunications companies, both local and international.

As CEO of Boundless Telecom, a Saudi Arabia-based business process outsourcing company, he was constantly on the move, planning the next big project for the company. This time, it was to establish a branch in the Philippines, in Iloilo City. This would be the third operations hub he would set up outside of KSA, in as many years.

It was a trip long overdue as well. Royce had not been in the Philippines for the better part of nine years.

Prince Khalid, his boss and the owner of Boundless, had urged him to take a break during his visit and charge his vacation expenses to the company. The prince's parting words, in a phone call before Royce flew out of Jeddah, still clung to the back of his mind.

You should think about getting married, too, my friend. Maybe now is the perfect time, after so many years of your hard work.

His phone rang, interrupting his thoughts. It was from his old Karate gym.

"Royce Duran."

"Good afternoon, Mr. Duran." The voice was warm. "This is Maggie. I'm calling to confirm that Miss Cisco has accepted your request for a one-on-one session tomorrow."

It was a shot in the dark, but her acceptance came as no surprise. Koreen Cisco was not the kind of woman who backed down from a challenge.

"Thank you. I'm sorry for such short notice. I'm glad she's accepted."

"You're welcome, sir. If you don't mind, please, Mr. Tuazon would like to speak with you."

Leo Tuazon, the son of the gym's owner and founder, had taken over since his parents retired.

"No problem, Maggie. Thanks again."

There was a brief rustle at the other end of the line, followed by a boisterous greeting.

"Royce, my man!"

"Hey, Leo. It's been a while."

"Yeah, it has. You know, we still have some of your old trophies displayed at the gym. My father never quite forgave you for leaving us to study in Manila. He lost a champion and a potential instructor."

Royce laughed. "He's still holding on to that grudge, isn't he?"

"Never got over it."

"How are your parents, though? Both good?"

Leo sighed. "Well, they're both doing okay. They prefer staying in the province these days. The city's gotten too crowded for them, I suppose. I do get them to go on Zoom when there's a promotion ceremony, just so they can see the kids."

"Ah, promotions. I remember those."

"I'm glad you're coming back tomorrow afternoon," said Leo enthusiastically. "And I'm even happier that you're reconnecting with Koreen. You two were the best we've ever had. No other club has ever had a year when they had two regional kata champions."

"Thanks for welcoming me back, Leo."

"Of course! And thank you for your generous donation to the gym. The new training equipment will make a huge difference."

"Anything to give back. Always happy to help out."

They spoke about the gym and its former students

and instructors for a few more minutes and exchanged goodbyes.

As he hung up the phone, Royce's thoughts drifted, inexorably, to Koreen.

What was her reaction to his request for a one-on-one? He wondered if she knew that he'd offered the gym double the charge of their usual sessions—and added a tip.

He'd seen her pictures on social media; she updated randomly and irregularly, mostly with pictures of inter-school math competitions, Karate tournaments, and the odd birthday greeting. She didn't seem to have much of a personal life.

Her brother, Kenneth, had been affectionately vocal on this.

"She's the same girl you knew, Royce. If anything, as a grown woman, she's more determined than ever."

He couldn't fault her for it.

If there was someone who understood ambition and drive very well, it was him.

His phone buzzed again, this time with a reminder for a conference call with the Boundless management team in Pune, India. It would be noontime there.

Performance data and notes on the Pune site had been linked to the reminder, too. With the amount of reports he could see, the meeting would take no less than two hours. His personal assistant, Yoshida, was nothing if not meticulous.

So much for reminiscing.

Royce's world moved too quickly sometimes. And he knew he'd built it in such a way that it didn't know how to wait, even for him.

His Saturdays were usually filled with informal meetings. Most of the time, he would have brunch with the prince or some of his contemporaries in Jeddah. These luxurious meals weren't technically downtime; casual conversations inevitably swirled towards business.

Sometimes, Royce would be travelling for a site visit, a conference, or a meeting out of town, to strike yet another deal. It was strange to wake up and not be concerned about getting ready to get to work, for a change.

He wasn't really certain if it was a welcome one.

That Saturday, he rose with a tight sensation in the pit of his stomach, far more pronounced than any tension he'd feel before potentially striking a deal worth millions of dollars.

The only meeting in his schedule that day meant far more than any contract won for Boundless.

The thought of seeing Koreen again was somewhat unnerving.

Did she still have his black belt?

They hadn't kept in touch much since their last meeting at the football field all those years ago, only occasionally seeing each other's updates online. Other than her liking a few of his posts, mostly pictures of work functions and events, their interactions had been very limited.

He'd lost count of how many times he had wanted to reach out to her before, even with just a message or a phone call, but something had always held him back. It was the unseen yet undeniably powerful wall that had always stood between them, time and distance be damned.

Their school and training days were long behind them,

but their belts, together in her keeping, still symbolized some kind of connection.

Or did they?

Perhaps this kind of sentimentality came with age, or the fact that he was back in a place he still considered his childhood home.

Instead of dwelling any further on his wandering thoughts, he glanced at his phone. Even though it was the weekend, there was always something at Boundless that needed his attention. Work didn't disappoint. He needed to answer a few emails.

Afterwards, he had breakfast at the hotel's poolside restaurant and visited the construction site of Boundless Tower, which wasn't far from where he was staying.

Once he got back to the hotel, he began to get ready for his training session with Koreen that afternoon.

It felt strange that, for the first time in his life, he didn't have the proper attire for Karate anymore. He'd long since outgrown his gi, kept with his old belongings at his parents' house in Manila.

Ordinary exercise gear would have to do. He was grateful he always brought gym attire whilst on travel. Squeezing in an hour or two for a workout was always a welcome respite from his hectic schedule.

He was zipping up his bag when his phone buzzed with a message. He glanced at the screen to find a text message from Kenneth Cisco.

"Hey man! How's Iloilo so far?"

He typed out a reply, trying to keep his tone neutral.

"Good. Saw the site for the Tower. Glad it hasn't rained since yesterday."

"Great! Koreen knows you're back, by the way."

Kenneth's words jumped out the screen.

The mention of her name in the message brought about an unexpected rush of nerves. Booking a training session with a phone call was one thing; being referred to by her own brother was something else entirely.

"Can't wait to catch up with you. Let me know about that basketball game. I'm meeting Wesley tomorrow for drinks."

It was the best response he could muster, without sounding too evasive.

As he waited for the car that would take him to his old Karate gym, he looked at his reflection in the closet's full-length mirror. He'd chosen to wear a simple black shirt and sweatpants.

Even in nondescript sportswear, he still looked formidable enough. He had grown to his full height of six feet by the time he turned twenty-one. Over the years, he'd put on at least sixty pounds of muscle on what used to be his lanky teenaged frame.

He still looked like someone worthy of Koreen Cisco's attention.

Mercifully, the phone rang.

"Your car is ready, Mr. Duran," the polite voice on the other end informed him.

"Thank you. I'm on my way down."

With a final glance at his reflection in the mirror, he took a deep breath, steadying himself for the encounter that awaited him.

It was time to step back onto the mat.

THREE

Koreen

REWIND

Her Saturdays were usually fueled by coffee and determination.

Today was no different, except there was a significant amount of anxiety thrown into the mix. She'd barely slept the night before.

At sunrise, Koreen gave up and got out of bed. She headed for the living room, to the shelf where her mother kept their awards and certificates along with a massive collection of framed photographs.

For the past fifteen years, she'd kept Royce's belt on the shelf next to her trophies and their picture together, taken moments after they had both been awarded their kata championships. She had never imagined the day would come that the belt would actually be returned to its owner.

She took out the canvas bag embroidered with his name, untouched after so many years. The black belt had been neatly folded inside, but there was something else she'd kept along with it.

In the thin light of dawn trickling through the windows, her fingers reached into the bag and settled on a piece of cardboard folded in half. She slid it out carefully and placed the canvas bag back onto the shelf.

It would be the first time in years she'd mustered enough courage to look at *it* again.

She could still remember the white anemone with its beautiful, colorful stripes. It had dried to a clump of thin, light brown petals that looked more like leaves, a piece of its original cardboard box the only thing holding it together.

The summer Royce had left for Manila, she had held on to his parting gift with the utmost care, guardedly and devotedly, until the flower had drooped over her hands. She'd then kept it and a piece of the box with his belt ever since.

They were all meant to be memories: the anemone, the belt, and Royce Duran. Nothing more.

She put the cardboard piece inside the frame with their photo, locked away in a time long past.

Koreen took the canvas bag and closed the shelf's glass door, determined to go on with the day as if it were any other.

Morning came and went too soon. After downing two cups of coffee and finishing a piece of toast her mother had practically force-fed her before leaving the house, she found herself outside Nelly's tailoring shop on the city's old Main Street.

She had asked the seamstress, who made the school's uniforms for decades now, to alter an extra karategi they had sewn for the Tuazon school. The outfit was originally meant for a Criminology major who was a kumite athlete, but he'd pulled out of a competition weeks ago due to an injury from his intensive police training.

Late yesterday afternoon, Koreen had decided to pay for the uniform in full, hoping it would be ready within the tight overnight window she'd given.

This karategi was for Royce.

She had looked up his photos on social media to get an idea of how much he had grown since high school, using her vast experience to gauge his uniform size. It felt strange, almost invasive, to see him living a glamorous, high-flying life in those photos.

A life so different from her own.

Koreen sighed inwardly. She felt old and, somehow, left behind.

She pushed her thoughts aside and entered the shop. "Good morning, Nelly."

The seamstress, sharp-eyed and ageless with neatly-coiffed gray hair, was already hard at work behind her sewing machine.

"Ah, Koreen!" The older woman flashed her a big smile as she got to her feet. "Good news, dear. The girls and I managed to finish everything last night, including your rush order."

She let out a sigh of relief. "Thank you so much. You're a lifesaver. I'm so sorry again for troubling you about that additional uniform at the last minute."

Nelly waved her apology aside. "You never ask for favors, so I was pretty sure this is very important to you."

Koreen could only nod, trying to ignore the flush rising up her neck.

Two of Nelly's assistants walked into the room, wheeling a large rack full of neatly-pressed children's karategi in various sizes. Moving with practiced ease, they took the uniforms off their hangers and folded them into big white boxes.

The seamstress reached for a much larger karategi hanging at the far end of the rack. Standing next to it, Koreen was practically swallowed by the sheer amount of fabric.

"This one is quite big," Nelly said appraisingly. "I was surprised when you said you wanted to buy out De Silva's competition gi and size it up even more. Who is this for, anyway?"

"It's for a former student of the gym. I'll be teaching him later today."

"Really?" Nelly raised an eyebrow, clearly intrigued. "Tell me more about this mystery man."

Koreen hesitated slightly before answering, hoping Nelly couldn't see the heat that had somehow found its way into her cheeks. "His name's Royce Duran. We were in the same class back in high school, and, well, we've trained together since we were kids. I'm pretty sure his old uniform's from here, too. He's worked in Saudi Arabia for years, but he's back in town for business of some kind."

Nelly's gaze was unwaveringly, unabashedly curious. "Interesting. Is he single?"

She shrugged, trying to hide her discomfort at the direction the conversation was taking. "I'm not sure, but that's really none of my business. I just need to make sure this karategi fits him. He was a kata champion once. We won our titles at the same tournament, the same year."

"Wow, very impressive. So nice of you to get this organized for him."

Nice wasn't exactly how she'd treated Royce Duran in the past, but Nelly didn't have to know that—or anything about their history, for that matter.

"Anyway, I should get going soon," Koreen said, changing the subject. "My class starts at one. Thank you again for your help, Nelly."

"Of course, anytime. Let's get all these boxes ready to go."

They watched the assistants finish their task of packing up the uniforms. Before they could close the last box with Royce's new karategi inside it, Koreen stepped forward, her stomach churning at the task she was about to do.

"Just a second, please." Before she lost her nerve, she retrieved the canvas case with his black belt from her handbag.

She carefully placed the embroidered fabric on top of the gleaming white uniform. "This belt belonged to him when we trained together. It's time to give it back to its owner."

Nelly smiled as she closed the box and gestured for her assistants to seal it. "Maybe that's not the only thing that belongs to him."

Koreen blushed but didn't respond, opting to act as if she didn't hear what the seamstress said. Instead, she bid Nelly goodbye and helped the assistants load the boxes into her car.

The drive to the gym was a blur, the gravity of that afternoon's session hanging above her head like a specter that refused to leave her alone.

She could still recall his parting words vividly.

"With the way we've trained together over the years, our belts belong together, too."

Before she realized it, she was in the parking area outside

the building. Leo and Maggie were already there, waiting for her and the uniforms to arrive. Their excitement was palpable as they chatted about Royce's upcoming visit.

"Royce made some generous donations for equipment, Koreen. We can finally buy a couple of those inflatable dummies the little kids could practice on." The hero-worship was evident in Leo's voice. "He even paid more than twice the usual rate for a one-on-one session with you. We really needed that money."

"I know, Leo," she replied gently, as she retrieved her bags from the passenger seat. The act of giving back to the gym was not entirely unexpected, but the fact that Royce had paid extra for a session with her seemed a little too much. "It's good news for the gym."

She couldn't fault Leo for agreeing to the session. The gym was struggling financially, largely because he had tried not to increase fees for their students, leaving barely enough money to keep the facility afloat.

"His company must be doing so well," chimed in Maggie, as she reached for some of the boxes in the backseat. "One of my cousins has already put in her job application online with Boundless. They seem to be hiring for a lot of positions."

"Can you imagine," Leo went on, his eyes sparkling, "both you and Royce performing a kata sequence together? I'd give an arm and a leg to see that!"

Koreen shook her head at his enthusiasm. "Let's not get ahead of ourselves."

Maggie raised an eyebrow as piles of boxes teetered precariously in her arms. "It's not every day we get two champions in the gym. You're both legends. This is the kind of thing that goes viral on the Internet."

"I'm too old for those, Maggie," she replied dismissively, trying to keep the conversation grounded.

But both Maggie and Leo pressed on, insisting that having her and Royce together, after all these years, under their gym's roof at the same time was truly a big deal.

"Fine, whatever you say," Koreen finally conceded, embarrassed at their excitement and keen not to be late for her first class. "Now, please help me unload these uniforms. I still need to change."

As she walked into the gym and got ready for her classes, the weight of seeing Royce again grew heavier in her mind with each passing second.

She steeled herself against the onslaught of uncertainty. She had her responsibilities to focus on. She was determined to face them all—and the man from her past, too—head-on, just as she always had.

Koreen's muscles ached as she walked around the mat of the gym's main training area. Sweat beaded her brow as the thick, humid air wafted in through the open windows. The few wall and ceiling fans installed around the facility offered very little relief against the sticky mid-afternoon heat.

Her class for primary-grade children was arguably the busiest and the most exhausting on the Tuazon school timetable, but she wouldn't have it any other way.

Ever since her arrival at the gym that day, she'd focused her thoughts and energy on her students, closely assessing their progress to distract herself from what awaited her later. Her heart swelled with pride when one of her shyest pupils, a nine-year-old girl, executed a flawless, perfectly targeted roundhouse kick.

At half past three, she thanked the athletes who came to her kata technique session and wished them good luck in their upcoming competition. As soon as they had all dispersed to go home or change in the locker rooms, she made her way to the gym's tiny staff room.

She couldn't deny she wasn't tired, but adrenaline coursed through her veins, making her feel almost giddy. It didn't help that she hadn't really eaten much today, except for that piece of toast this morning.

She sat down on a plastic stool and took a minute to force down a banana and a small bottle of water. Her stomach rumbled in protest. She had no time or desire to eat anything more substantial.

Peeling off her damp karategi, Koreen took a deep breath for the first time in hours. She slipped into a fresh uniform, pulling the gi taut across her shoulders. As she arranged her hair into a neat bun, she caught a glimpse of herself in the mirror. The reflection staring back at her still held traces of the champion she once was—someone fierce, powerful, and unstoppable.

She emerged from the staff room at ten minutes to four. Another class was in full swing, led by Ace, a fellow instructor who worked at a nearby merchant marine school. She paused for a minute to watch the mid-level teenaged students as they attacked and defended in turn through their shadow-sparring exercises.

Other than the people in the class, the gym was empty. Older students usually didn't have parents or guardians hovering nearby. Maggie's desk at reception was deserted, and Leo had disappeared as well.

"God, I've missed doing this."

At the sound, her heart leaped into her throat. The words were spoken softly, meant only for her ears. Before she even laid eyes on him, she knew who the owner of the voice was.

Royce Duran's presence was undeniably imposing, as always. This time, she had to look way up to see his face.

He had always been athletic and strong, but now he stood before her as a man fully grown, the difference between their sizes and stature more significant and pronounced than ever. It was clear that he had continued to train and develop his body through the years.

His hair was shorter than before, now looking much like a crew cut. He had a very thin, perfectly-trimmed beard and mustache that gave him an exotic, intimidating air.

But it was his eyes that, as always, commanded her attention.

Even after fifteen years, she was familiar with his eyes, as if she'd last looked into them yesterday. Royce Duran's eyes had the deadly, unyielding focus of a seasoned predator.

Those same eyes were now smiling down at her.

"It's nice to see you, Koreen." His voice was deeper than she remembered.

She was at a loss for words. Her hands clenched into fists as she attempted to regain her composure.

"It's good you're on time, Duran." Her response came out colder than she'd intended it to sound.

It was as if she had some kind of standoffish reflex when it came to talking to him. She could still remember herself telling him on their high school's football field that agreeing to meet him was weird. She'd never realized, until it was too late, that he'd only wanted to say a proper goodbye.

"Wouldn't miss this for the world." His response was warm, almost friendly. "How have you been?"

"I'm fine," she replied, a little too quickly for her own comfort. "Busy as always, but fine. And you?"

His gaze never left her face as he answered. "It's good to be back in Iloilo. It's even better to be back in the gym after such a long time. I didn't realize how much I missed being here."

She was the first to break eye contact, averting her attention to the sparring teenagers in Ace's class. "Welcome back."

"Thank you. I'm glad you agreed to this session at such short notice. Starting Monday, I have meetings lined up, so this weekend is really the only one I've got free before all the craziness starts."

"Craziness?"

"Ah, yes." He chuckled softly. The sound sent shivers down her spine. "I'm back in town for business. I'm setting up a new operations center for my company, Boundless Telecom. We're planning to house an army of agents at a dedicated facility, providing translation and transcription services to clients in Europe and the Americas."

She nodded. "Sounds like a big venture. I could recommend a few of my trainees based in the city if you're looking for people to hire. They're hardworking, disciplined, and quick learners."

"Always teaching, aren't you?" There was an unmistakable smile in his voice.

"It just sort of fell into place. When my father died shortly after I started college, I found work in some BPO places to help my mother out."

"I'm very sorry about your father," he said, his tone now serious and sincere to her ears. "He'd always been kind to me. I'd never forget how well he could make a kite out of newspapers and barbecue sticks."

"Thanks."

Side by side, in strangely companionable silence, they watched the students in the class wrap up their sparring exercises.

Koreen glanced up at the clock. "It's time for us to train. Are you ready?"

"Always."

The way he said that one word seemed to hold a deeper meaning than merely being prepared for their session.

It didn't matter what he meant. She squared her shoulders and inclined her head towards the other side of the gym, a smaller enclosed training space that Leo had booked for their session.

As she looked up into his eyes, she could feel her heart hammering against her ribcage with equal parts anticipation and trepidation.

There it was, back from the dead: the familiar competitive fire within her began to burn—bright and undeniable.

"Alright, we'll see what you've got. Let's get started."

FOUR

Royce

RESURFACE

He looked around the gym where he'd spent countless hours training as a child and as a teenaged boy.

Royce had come in for his session early, unnoticed by all with the exception of Leo Tuazon, who had fawned over him a little too much. It had been a surreal experience, to see his martial arts school almost the same as it was before.

Seeing Koreen, however, was the most unsettling experience of all.

She had always been petite, but now she barely made it to his shoulder. She still kept her black hair long, piled high on top of her head. He'd always had the opinion that all she needed was a crown to complete the appearance of a warrior queen. Her brown eyes, cat-like and unapologetically intelligent, looked as determined as ever.

The fifteen years that stretched out between them seemed to have wavered; the gap it had created strangely closing, as if no time had passed.

"Lead the way," he replied, lowering his head slightly in a gesture of respect.

Koreen nodded, seemingly satisfied with his response. She brushed past him and made her way to a smaller, partially enclosed training area, the same place where they had both practiced their kata all those years ago.

He could see his younger self, standing beside her, their eyes locked in the mirror. There had always been an unspoken challenge between them as to who could deliver the sequences more flawlessly, more precisely.

Out of earshot of the ongoing class across the floor, she paused by the threshold. He'd expected her to bow before entering, as was custom. Instead, she crossed her arms over her chest and gave him a once-over.

"Before we get started, I want to know what kind of martial arts training you've been doing."

Somehow, her question made him feel vulnerable, almost inferior.

"I've barely done any Karate training since I went abroad. I did dabble in Taekwondo in college, but even then, I've always been drawn to Karate more. Maybe because I've studied it since I was four."

"I can understand why," she replied, nodding. "I tried training in Sanda, too, in another gym, after high school. I came back to Karate eventually. It felt like…home to me, I suppose."

He was surprised at how agreeable he and Koreen seemed at the moment. He didn't want to push his luck, but perhaps they had both matured over the years.

"Which brings us both back here, now." He gave her a small smile.

Instead of smiling back, she raised an eyebrow and looked him up and down again, shaking her head disapprovingly. "Is that what you're planning to wear for our session?"

"Uh, yeah," he replied, glancing down at his sports attire, slightly taken aback by her question. "I don't have a karategi anymore. I outgrew my old one a long time ago."

Koreen's lips formed a thin line as she shook her head. "That's unacceptable. Follow me."

Before he could respond, she led him to a locker near the changing rooms. She opened the tiny steel door and gestured to a karategi hanging inside. It was a pristine white, adorned with the logos and colors of the Tuazon school.

"This is for you, Duran," she said, gesturing to the uniform. Her chin was lifted, but her gaze seemed focused on something above his shoulder. "Take it."

Too surprised to say anything, he reached inside the locker as instructed and pulled the karategi out. It became clear that the uniform was tailored perfectly to his size.

"Koreen, how did you...?" His voice trailed off as his mind raced to find the right words to show his appreciation. Their history together made it difficult for him to express his gratitude—or any other emotion.

But she wasn't finished. From the same locker, she produced a small canvas bag. He could see his name embroidered on the worn fabric.

It was his black belt.

"Here. It's time you have it back."

Time seemed to stand still as his mind flashed back to their awkward farewell at the football field fifteen years ago. He had so much left unsaid back then. Even until now…he still didn't have the words.

He reached out to take the belt from her, and when their hands touched, he didn't pull away this time. Instead, he squeezed her hands gently.

Koreen's hands seemed smaller and more delicate, but no less powerful.

"Thank you." It was all he could say.

"It's the least I could do, to honor a former champion of the school." The expression on her face was unreadable.

He let her hands go but found himself unable to look away from her eyes.

She was the one who took the step back.

All of the sudden, he felt it.

It was the same thing that had always stopped him from reaching out to her on social media—the very thing that had prevented him from calling out her name across the field.

"It will only take a minute for me to change," he said instead.

"Good."

Without another word, she turned and walked away.

The invisible barrier between them had asserted itself, once more.

He wasn't certain if the mirror was lying or not, but Royce liked what he saw.

He had no idea how Koreen had managed to estimate his size with such precision. The new karategi fitted him perfectly, the fabric falling against the lines of his body as if it knew exactly what kind of movements to expect from his limbs.

With the black belt tied just above his hip line, he looked as if he'd always belonged in the uniform.

As if he had never left.

He took a deep breath and exited the men's locker room, quickly making his way back to the enclosed training area.

She was waiting for him, standing in the middle of the room with her hands clasped behind her back.

"Wow." He took in the familiar sight of the mirrored walls and the dark blue rubber mats on the floor. "This place hasn't changed much."

"Leo replaced the mats a few years ago, but that's about it," Koreen said in a quiet voice. "The business barely makes any money, but he's trying not to increase the fees for the students."

He'd thought as much, the moment he'd seen the weather-worn sign outside and the slightly dilapidated state of the office furniture in the gym's reception area.

"Stubborn just like his parents, huh?"

She smiled; it was a tentative upward curving of her lips, but it was enough for him.

"Yeah. I suppose Ace, Jonah, and I are just as stubborn. We refuse to leave him."

Leo had pointed Ace out earlier on the floor. Royce didn't know him, but he knew Jonah. She was a few years older than he and Koreen, and a kumite champion back in the day.

He chuckled. "To keep a place like this running, he needs people like you. He's very lucky you're all with him."

She didn't respond, but her eyes searched the room before finally settling on him.

"So, what's your goal for this session, Duran?"

He hesitated for a moment before answering honestly. "My goal was to see you."

Her eyebrows shot up, and various expressions flickered across her face in quick succession: surprise, confusion, curiosity. "What do you mean?"

"Exactly that," he replied with a shrug. "To see you. To train with you, like before."

She regarded him silently for a moment before she spoke. "Alright, then. You need to warm up first. We'll start with some kata sequences once you're ready."

He stood before her and bowed, indicating he was at her bidding. As she rattled off a series of exercises for him to do, he watched her face closely.

Just like before, he couldn't tell what she was thinking. Was she pleased by his admission, or did it make her uncomfortable?

As he began his warm-up, she watched him wordlessly, her eyes tracking his every movement. The rest of her looked as elegant and stoic as a marble statue.

The gym echoed with the sound of other students practicing their own techniques, but he didn't really pay much attention to anything else. As he moved under the watchful eye, her opinion of him was the only thing that mattered.

His muscles ached as he finished the warm-up, sweat trickling down his face and back. He looked over at her, trying to gauge her reaction.

"You're in pretty good shape for a man your age," she told him bluntly.

"Thanks," he replied, wiping sweat from his brow, unwilling to admit he was one burpee away from collapsing. "But you look to be in way better shape than me. I guess a good kata sequence would prove my point."

If he knew her well enough from their shared childhood and youth, he might still be able to push a few of her buttons.

She didn't disappoint.

Koreen hesitated for a moment, this time her eyes flashing and narrowing in turn. She looked slightly uncomfortable, as if he'd crossed an invisible line.

"I'm better now," she bit out. "Better than I used to be."

Her reaction—and her words—gave him immense satisfaction.

"Only one way to find out, isn't there?"

This time, she took the bait, almost hungrily. "Why don't you do the entire sequence with me, then, Duran? I assume you still remember Pinan One to Eight?"

"I'll try," he responded with downcast eyes. "I'm sure I'll remember if you're by my side."

She turned to face the wall-length mirror and gestured for him to take his position to her left.

As they stood side by side, Royce marveled at how little had changed between them. Time had not faded the way they both held themselves, the intensity that radiated from each of them.

"Get ready." Her words cut through the still, tense air between them like a knife.

His eyes met hers in the mirror. "Before we begin, if I do the entire sequence perfectly, I owe you dinner for being such a fantastic sensei."

She seemed taken aback by his comment, but before she

could respond, Maggie walked into the room, carrying a towel and a bottle of water.

"Are you going to do the kata?" Maggie asked, her mouth dropping open in surprise. "Together?"

Koreen shot her a pointed look, but confirmed with a terse, wordless nod.

Excited, Maggie called out for Leo, announcing that they had to take a video of this.

"Our two champions, guys!" Her voice rang throughout the gym.

Maggie's enthusiasm was highly contagious; soon, Ace and his class of teenagers had gathered around the enclosed area, eager to witness the showdown.

Royce's heart hammered in his chest as he glanced around the room, taking in the sea of faces before him. He could count at least forty people; more than half of them already had mobile phones in their hands, cameras trained towards him and Koreen.

He swallowed hard, feeling a tight knot of anxiety forming in his stomach. Speaking before the Board of Directors of Boundless was nothing compared to this.

This was not what he had expected when he'd challenged Koreen to perform the kata sequence with him. But now, he knew there was no turning back.

With a deep breath, he met Koreen's gaze in the mirror, finding quiet challenge and a resigned determination in her eyes. She leaned closer, her voice barely audible above the excited murmurs of their audience. "Don't you dare let me and this school down."

She moved to resume her preparatory stance, but paused

midway and tilted her head to the side. "Besides, you're a champion, aren't you, Duran?"

If he knew how to push her buttons, she knew how to push his, too. It was an exchange as old as time.

"Wouldn't dream of disappointing you," he whispered back.

"We'll find out soon enough," she said simply, straightening. "Let's begin."

As they bowed and started the kata sequence at her command, he pushed all thought aside, focusing instead on Koreen's graceful form beside him.

They still moved in sync, their bodies mirroring each other's strikes, blocks and kicks. Over the years, he'd done this sequence countless times on his own, just to make sure he never forgot. It connected him to this place, to his childhood, and, most importantly, to her.

This time, it felt very different with a live audience, in his old martial arts school no less.

It felt very different with Koreen by his side.

As they progressed through the steps, Royce felt the strain in his muscles, his body slick with sweat from the exertion. He knew he couldn't falter; the stakes had never been higher. He wasn't just performing for an audience, or even a score.

He was performing for himself—and for her.

By the time they reached the end of the sequence, his knees trembled and his breath came in ragged gasps. But he stood tall, refusing to show any sign of weakness, after they took the final bow to mark the end of Pinan Eight.

Before she could react, he stepped forward, filling the space before her.

He bowed deeply, making sure he never lost eye contact

even as he made the ultimate gesture of respect, humility, and gratitude.

"Sensei," he said, the single word carrying the weight of everything left unsaid between them.

The gym erupted into cheers and applause, the sound deafening in its intensity.

He didn't move until she bowed back.

Only then did he straighten and turn to face the rest of the room, smiling and bowing to an audience he didn't quite see.

All he could see before him were the years falling away.

The raw, undeniable bond between him and the woman who had always been his equal—and, oftentimes, superior—in so many ways.

The fierce battle for supremacy that had always seemed to divide their world into two.

For now, he was certain, whatever it was that connected and separated them in equal measure, had never truly faded.

FIVE

Koreen

RESTART

"Excuse me, Miss Cisco?" Koreen looked up from the stack of quiz papers she was grading. It was late afternoon. All the other teachers had left for the day. She was savoring a rare moment of solitude in the faculty room before going to the gym later for her grueling Thursday night kumite class.

One of her senior students in Modern Algebra had poked his head through the half-open doorway. He was wearing a school jersey, probably still at practice in the courts near her office. "Yes, Paul? How can I help you?"

"There's someone asking for you. He said he was a classmate of yours."

"He's here?" The words escaped her mouth before she

could stop herself. She had forgotten about Royce's dinner offer.

That wasn't entirely correct. She had tried very hard not to think about him or their on-the-spot kata demonstration at the gym that past weekend.

If not for Leo, Ace, and the students present, she would have walked out right then and there. Royce had expertly goaded her into accepting a challenge she had no business considering from the very start.

She was an instructor, fourth dan black. She should not have allowed herself to fall for his bait of doing the kata with him, especially to a live audience, most of them with camera phones in hand. She was supposed to have more dignity and restraint than that. Kata was meant to be sacred, not the object of a random challenge or something to post on the Internet.

"Hey, Paul. Is your Ma'am Cisco in there?" She heard a deeper, older male voice coming from the corridor.

Paul's head disappeared from sight. "Yup. She's right in there, Mister Duran."

A few more words were exchanged, before she heard a set of receding footsteps.

"Good afternoon, ma'am." It was Royce's turn to poke his head through the doorway. "Although you look more like a student, I'm getting a very strange sense of *déjà vu* right now."

She glared at him. "Did you come all the way here just to throw jabs at my age?"

"Not really, considering I'm two months older," he answered, deadpan, walking into the room. "I tried calling and sending you messages. I thought I might have gotten your number wrong, but Kenneth told me it was correct."

There was nothing wrong with the number he'd been

calling or texting. She had deliberately avoided his calls and not opened any of the messages he'd sent. She had known it was him trying to reach her since Monday; she'd gotten his number from Maggie's records.

His session had been completed. He was supposed to be busy now, wasn't he? He should just carry on with his business in town and leave her alone.

She shrugged. "I must have been busy at the time. Would you like to have a seat?"

She gestured to the chair in front of her desk. Regardless of what she felt at seeing him again and her reaction to last Saturday's events, she didn't want to appear rude.

"Thanks." He strode into the room, his presence dwarfing everything else in sight.

It was a presence that was impossible to ignore.

Today, he wasn't in sports attire. Instead, he had on a perfectly cut aqua-colored polo shirt and dark blue slacks. His feet were encased in what looked like black leather boots, shiny and expensive-looking. He looked sleek, but understated enough not to be ostentatious.

Royce had always held himself with quiet dignity, which made him appear more mature than most of their peers. As a man, he moved with more confidence. He looked like someone with the world at his command.

Maybe it was.

He settled gracefully in the chair in front of her desk, tilting his head to look at the papers she was marking. "Algebra?"

She nodded. "Modern Algebra. I also teach Trigonometry and Calculus."

"Always teaching."

"Yeah."

She finished grading the quiz paper, and looked up. Her breath hitched the moment they locked gazes. It was as if he'd never taken his eyes off her the moment he walked into the room.

"What brings you here? I think I'm the only teacher left around for the day, except maybe Coach Porras."

"I saw him when I came in. He's the one who asked Paul to take me here."

"I can schedule a visit for you, if you like."

He shook his head. "That's not why I'm here. I came to see you, to make good on my dinner invitation."

His words at the gym echoed in the back of her head.

"My goal was to see you."

She didn't know what to make of it. Competing against the younger Royce Duran was easy. Dealing with the gentleman who had taken his place was something else—something very unnerving.

"I thought you were joking." Koreen sighed and shook her head. "I honestly believed you didn't mean any of it."

"I meant what I said. I'm sorry if you thought I was trying to pull some kind of stunt on you. At our age, we should have already outgrown whatever bad blood we had between us by now."

She put down her pen and pushed the papers on her desk to one side. This was not the kind of conversation she wanted to have, much less in the faculty room of all places.

"It's not bad blood. It's not even about whatever's between us."

"Then what's this about?"

"You. Your intentions." She got to her feet as soon as she uttered the words. Sitting behind the desk felt suffocating all of a sudden. She had to put some distance between them; at least she should be relieved that she still had enough energy to move.

It was strange to see him looking up at her. "My intentions?"

"Why are you doing this?"

"As I said, I wanted to see you."

"Why?"

"We haven't seen each other in fifteen years. Besides, it's not every day someone goes out of their way to get a karategi done for me, much less a perfect one. I have not even thanked you properly for that—or for keeping my belt all these years. I'm just trying to be friendly."

They had been rivals, competitors, training partners. Never friends.

There had always been a line between them—an invisible divide that bisected the world.

That is, until he said goodbye fifteen years ago.

Until the anemone he'd given her—the first flower she'd ever received from a boy—wilted and fell apart in her fingers.

Her pride would never, ever allow her to admit that she'd cried that night. In the morning, she'd cut a piece of the black cardboard box and stashed the petals inside it, to be kept along with his belt in the years to come.

"You don't have to thank me," she replied, stepping away from her own desk. She tried to avoid looking into his eyes, but couldn't help it. "You don't owe me anything."

He regarded her with an unreadable expression on his face, his dark eyes unblinking. "On the contrary."

"What makes you say that?"

"Last Saturday, when I first saw you, you gave me the best

business epiphany I've ever had in years. Without knowing it, you managed to solve a very big problem of mine, in the space of a single conversation."

Koreen shook her head. All those years working so hard abroad had probably unhinged him. "What the hell are you talking about?"

"Boundless Tower is our biggest operations site to date, and we need the best person to run it. I believe you would be that person."

This was the last thing she had ever expected him to say.

"I want to offer you the position of Country Manager," Royce continued, a little more animatedly. "To oversee the place as it is built and supervise the operations once everything is up and running."

A job, she thought dazedly, finally managing to piece together the meaning of his words. *A very big, important job.*

Managing Boundless Tower in her own hometown would be a far cry from having her own tiny BPO training center. At this stage in her life, she could barely afford a single whiteboard with her savings, much less the computers, peripherals, and software required. She didn't even want to think about how much it would cost to rent a decent facility.

It was the biggest possible shock he could have sprung on her. So much so, that all she could do was stare at him, dumbstruck.

"What made you think that?" she finally asked, cautiously, aware that her voice was shaking.

He shrugged. "The Tower in Iloilo will be one of Southeast Asia's biggest and most advanced outsourcing facilities. If I had to trust my dreams and lifeblood with someone, it would be the smartest, hardest working person I know. You."

She shook her head. "You're crazy."

"There's no one like you, Koreen. Let me make that very clear. I knew a little bit about your background in the industry, but when I found out you were training people as well, it just clicked." Royce stood up slowly, his gaze never leaving her face. "I was going to make you the offer over dinner, under circumstances much better than this."

For the longest time, and she could never really fathom how long, they both stood in the middle of the faculty room, wordlessly sizing each other up.

"I need some time to think about it," she heard herself say, after what seemed like the longest pause. "If that's what you're really asking."

"Yes, it is. Take all the time you need. I'll be around for at least a few months if you want to clarify anything. You have my number, don't you?"

She flushed as she nodded, the meaning behind his seemingly casual question clear. He knew she had been avoiding his calls and messages. Time and distance seemed not to have diminished Royce Duran's ability to get into her head and under her skin.

"I'll have my assistant message you the link to a private folder with the job description and offer. There will be some forms for you to complete, too, once you decide to accept the offer."

"Great." The single word escaped her awkwardly. Somehow, she felt cornered and embarrassed, like a child caught in a blatant lie by a grown-up. He still had the talent for effortlessly one-upping her, even as an adult. "Looking forward to it."

"Thank you."

"You're welcome."

He gave her a smile. "So, what about dinner? Does tomorrow sound good?"

For a moment, she considered refusing his invitation, but she couldn't think of a good enough excuse, considering he had just offered her a job that most people could only dream of. The sooner she had dinner with him, the sooner she could go on with her simple, straightforward, hectic life.

"I have a class at the training center until seven-thirty."

"I'll pick you up after, if you don't mind sending me the location."

"I'll do that."

Before she knew what he was doing, before she could step away, Royce had closed the distance between them. "I promise, no business talk. I'm glad I got that over with today."

He was so close she could have sworn she could hear his heart beating loudly, or maybe it was her own. She wasn't quite sure which, but, at that moment, she was more concerned with catching her own breath.

This was no longer the same Royce Duran from fifteen years ago. This older, stronger, bigger version was decidedly harder to deal with.

But she was still Koreen Cisco, wasn't she? She could always handle him.

She stood straight, lifting her chin until they were eye to eye. "I'll see you tomorrow, then."

His grin caught her off-guard as he echoed her earlier response. "Looking forward to it."

SIX

Royce

RECALL

THE NIGHT WAS HUMID, THE AIR THICK WITH A heaviness that settled on his skin as he stood outside the training center. The wind whipped around him, carrying with it the sharp scent of impending rain. It was almost eight in the evening. Across the road, the car from the hotel and its driver idled patiently.

Royce watched as the trainees trickled out after their classes, laughing and talking, discussing weekend plans and job applications. He smiled inwardly when he heard one of them mention that he and a few friends were applying for jobs at the new Boundless Tower.

As the number of students exiting the building began to dwindle, he approached a group of girls.

"Excuse me, ladies, do any of you happen to know Miss Cisco?"

The trio looked him over, eyes wide with curiosity. They nudged each other, giggling, as if to determine which of them had to respond to his question.

Finally, one girl managed to shush the other two, long enough for her to answer. "Yes, she's our trainer. We just finished our class."

"Why are you asking?" another girl chimed in, before she was elbowed.

"I'm waiting for Miss Cisco," he replied smoothly, with what he hoped was a reassuring smile. "I thought perhaps she had forgotten about me."

"She actually dismissed our session five minutes early," said the first girl. "But she asked us to stay behind."

"Wait, are you her boyfriend?" The third girl's eyes were alight with what looked like mischief as she exchanged knowing glances with the others. "We helped her get ready…for your date."

"See?" The second girl looked as if she had just hit the jackpot, her grin almost reaching her ears. "I told you she's got a hot date. Good thing we convinced her to let us do her makeup!"

"Wow," murmured the third girl, eyeing him up and down.

"She should be out soon," said the first girl, her eyes shooting daggers at her companions. Without another word, she grabbed her friends' hands and pulled them away.

A chorus of excited chatter followed the girls as they walked off into the night, disappearing into the shadows as the lights of the building began to go out one by one.

Royce resumed his wait, amused and bemused at his encounter with Koreen's students.

Offering her the job as manager of the Philippine operations of Boundless was a bold move, but she was perfect for it—someone he could trust completely. Her passionate, persistent, determined nature had been a constant ever since they were children. She was the kind of person who put her heart and soul into everything she did.

There was no denying how much he admired her for it. Or admired *her*.

Regardless of what he felt, he hoped she would accept the job. The idea of having her in his life again was a welcome one.

In an almost dreamlike haze, he saw her emerge from the building. Carrying a simple black bag, she was dressed in a shimmery black dress and strappy heels. The dress hugged her body, while her long hair cascaded around her shoulders in soft curls. Her cat-like eyes were even more striking with the makeup she wore; her full lips were painted an enticing, deep shade of red.

His breath caught in his throat; his heart pounded so hard he felt as if he'd been punched, thrown, and kicked all at once.

Fuck.

Desire coursed through him, undeniable and strong in its sudden intensity, leaving him momentarily disoriented.

He could only think of two words.

So beautiful.

She had always been a strikingly attractive girl, but the Koreen who now stood before him, with a somewhat concerned expression on her face, was on another level entirely.

"Duran?" Her voice carried a hint of uncertainty. He

probably looked like a big, bumbling idiot. Hell, maybe he was even drooling.

He was grateful there wasn't that much light left for her to see him clearly. He was surprised, to put it mildly, and highly aroused. All he wanted to do was take her in his arms and maybe to his hotel room. In reality, if he tried, she'd probably put him in the hospital with a few well-placed strikes.

Forcing himself to focus, he stepped forward with a smile. "Koreen, you look stunning tonight."

"Thank you." Even the sparse light could not disguise the blush tainting her cheeks.

"Here, let me take your bag." He offered his hand, and she hesitated for just a moment before surrendering it.

Unable to resist, he bent down to kiss her cheek, inhaling the fruity scent of her perfume. He braced himself for a punch or a sharp retort, but it didn't come. Instead, she placed her hand on his shoulder, returning his kiss, her lips warm against his skin.

"Are you ready to go?" It took all of his self-control to keep his voice steady.

She nodded, her thumb grazing his cheek. He realized she was wiping away a trace of her lipstick. "Yes, I am."

He took her hand and, together, they crossed the road to the waiting car.

The car pulled up to the grand entrance of Royce's hotel, its opulent architecture even more dazzling under the warm lights of the building façade.

"This place is incredible," Koreen murmured, her eyes

wide as she took in the sights before her. "I could never afford something like this on a teacher's salary."

"Consider it my treat." He smiled at her, feeling a sense of pride in being able to share this luxury.

As they stepped out of the car and made their way to the grand lobby, he noticed the appreciative glances she drew from other guests and staff alike. A feeling akin to pride swelled within him.

She was a rare gem. Strong, smart, and beautiful. No wonder he had found his way back to her, after all these years.

The hotel manager greeted them warmly as they approached the bank of elevators.

"Your table at the poolside restaurant is ready, Mr. Duran," he said, shaking Royce's hand. "We have also prepared a backup option indoors should the weather take a turn for the worse. There are reports of heavy rains and potentially a storm coming later tonight or early morning."

"Thank you," Royce responded. "I just hope the weather wouldn't affect the progress of the Tower's construction too much."

The manager nodded. "Let's hope so, sir. For what it's worth, I'm glad you chose this area to build your project on. We have the least flooding in the city proper. That's why our owners chose to have the hotel here as well. It's one of the safest places to be."

The manager led them out to the poolside restaurant, where the staff whisked them off to a prime table situated close to the water. The subtle glow of the pool lights reflected off Koreen's glimmering dress, giving her an ethereal appearance that made his heart race. He wanted nothing more than to touch her, to make sure she was really there with him.

To make sure that she was the same girl he'd known since they were both four years old.

"Please, have a seat." He pulled out her chair, ignoring the two waiters hovering nearby. He was going to stay as close as he possibly could to her, everyone else be damned. She sat down gracefully, her eyes never leaving his as he took his own seat across from her.

"Would you like something to drink?" he offered, gesturing for their waiter.

She looked at the drinks menu on the table before her, shaking her head a little bit. "I'm not much of a drinker. I don't even go out very often. Too busy."

Her sheepish admittance made him laugh. "Don't worry, I'm much worse. I don't even have time to go out. I only drink socially, outside of Saudi. Sharia Law prohibits alcohol."

They settled on mocktails, a decision that seemed to make her relax visibly.

"I've noticed from your social media that you travel a lot," she said, her cheeks flushing as she realized how that might sound. "I mean, for work, obviously."

He reached across the table to pat her hand reassuringly. "Yes, I do travel quite a bit," he admitted, surprised when she didn't pull away from his touch. "It's part of the job, but it also gives me the chance to experience different cultures and meet new people. And eat a lot of food."

She smiled. "I can see that. If you didn't quit martial arts, you could easily get a job in the WWE."

He grinned right back. "Never too late to consider a career change as a pro wrestler, then?"

She regarded him seriously. "You might last a few good

years, give or take, if you get back into training. But that's only my opinion, in case you get bored of the high-flying CEO life."

"Tell me about your work, Koreen," he encouraged, leaning back in his chair and sipping his mocktail. "Kenneth mentioned you're always on the go."

"He did, huh?"

"The kid's quite proud of you. He could only hope to have half of your determination. Hospital residencies are not for the faint of heart."

"He's learning," Koreen relented grudgingly. "But he's still got a long way to go."

"But you've gone all the way and back, haven't you?"

"You mean aside from teaching at the high school, gym, and training center?"

He nodded.

"That's just the bare minimum. I tutor kids in Math on Sundays, and I do one-on-one sessions in Karate whenever I could. Sometimes, I get invitations to teach BPO courses remotely, too."

"It sounds like you genuinely enjoy teaching, don't you?"

She nodded enthusiastically. "I do. It's the idea of helping someone learn something new and amazing that keeps me going. Once they have the knowledge, it can't be taken away."

He watched her entire face glow as she spoke about teaching. He had never seen someone so passionate and breathtaking, all at the same time.

"My dream is to have my own BPO training center someday," Koreen continued, a touch of wistfulness in her voice. "Maybe one that's subsidized, so kids with less money can afford it and still find work in the industry."

"At Boundless, as its country manager, you would have so

much more," Royce said, allowing business to creep into their conversation, unable to help but put his best offer forward. "You could give more people opportunities like that. This is the very reason why we chose Iloilo instead of any other city for our third international operations center. The potential of the local talent is incredibly high and, of course, this place will always be my hometown."

He quickly caught himself and added, raising his hands in mock surrender, "I promise not to mention anything business-related anymore tonight."

"It's okay." She smiled, seemingly relieved. "So, have you visited your old house or seen any of your old friends while you've been here?"

"Actually, my old house has been demolished along with a few others to make way for apartments. But yes, I've managed to catch up with Wesley and Owen over the past week. I'm looking forward to seeing Kenneth and some of the old basketball gang maybe next weekend. He told me he'd asked for a few days off."

Just as they were settling into a comfortable rhythm in their conversation, the waiter arrived to take their order.

Koreen hesitated and glanced at him, clearly uncomfortable with the expensive menu. "Go ahead, pick for me, please."

Royce took over smoothly, ordering starters and mains while telling the waiter they would consider dessert later. As they were left alone again, he felt the time was right to address the earlier moment of honesty between them.

"I meant what I said yesterday," he said quietly, leaning a little closer to see the reaction on her face. "I was telling you the truth."

"What truth?" she replied cautiously, her eyes searching his face.

"That the reason I'm here is to see you." He held on to her gaze as he spoke, to make sure she wouldn't see him falter. "I couldn't come back to Iloilo and not see you. It's been such a long time…and this dinner is long overdue."

Her surprise was unmistakable; she drew back into her chair slightly as she visibly paled at his declaration. He didn't want to make her uncomfortable, but he would rather be honest to someone like Koreen Cisco. She deserved no less.

"The last time we saw each other, we were kids," came her measured response. "We didn't know anything back then."

"Maybe a thing or two," he responded with a smile. "We should give ourselves more credit. Once upon a time, we were unstoppable."

She returned his smile hesitantly. "What do you want, then, Duran? Can I even give it?"

He welcomed such bluntness. It made her special. "Can we start over as adults, become friends? We have too much history to ignore, don't we? We practically grew up together."

"Friends," she echoed, her fingers playing with the edge of the tablecloth, eyes fluttering open and shut as if her thoughts were on rapid fire. "I'd like that. We're too old to try and keep one-upping each other all the time."

"I can't entirely promise the not one-upping each other part," he replied, relieved. "It's become too much of a habit."

A light, almost carefree laugh escaped her lips. He found himself mesmerized by the sound. He reached out across the table and, this time, took her hand in his with a gentle squeeze.

"You should smile and laugh more, Sensei. It makes you even more beautiful."

She blushed and dismissed the compliment with a wave of her free hand. "Come on, Duran. You don't need to flatter me. You know it wouldn't work."

"Trust me, I'm not flattering you. I'm surprised there's no one around to beat the shit out of me when I asked you to join me for dinner."

Her cheeks turned a deeper shade of pink as she shook her head. "I've been single for a long time. I'm too busy. There's no time for a relationship."

"I see." Royce felt an even deeper sense of relief at her words, understanding only too well the challenge of balancing one's professional and personal lives. "I can relate. I suppose we have chosen our paths, haven't we?"

The meaning between them was not lost, as they stared at each other across the table, the already humid air thickening with tension. Before either could say anything more, their exchange was interrupted by the arrival of their food. The waiter set plates filled with colorful dishes in front of them, the mouthwatering scents wafting through the sharp evening air.

"Thank you," he said to the waiter, who nodded and retreated discreetly. Turning back to Koreen, he gestured to the feast before them. "Please go ahead and begin, Sensei."

She nodded and smiled in return, letting his hand go to pick up her fork, but not without giving it a squeeze first, making his breath catch again.

Even as they began to eat, he couldn't deny the almost palpable electric current running between them, a spark reignited from a childhood rivalry forged years ago, now transformed into something else entirely.

SEVEN

Koreen

REMNANT

She sipped the last few drops of her coffee, taking in the sight of him.

All evening long, Royce had been relaxed and attentive, and so effortlessly funny. She had never really seen him that way before. Then again, she had never really spent any time with him before, not like tonight.

He was only supposed to be someone from her past; a boy who'd been a constant presence in a childhood long gone, now a man of power and wealth meant to be a distant, glittering presence on her social media feed. He wasn't supposed to be seated from across her, much less touching her hand as if they had been friends for years.

The way he looked at her, however, was a different matter.

Under his gaze, Koreen felt both self-conscious and wanted, vulnerable and powerful.

"Are you ready to head home?" He put down his own cup on the table and gestured for the waiter to take the bill folder.

Around them, the restaurant was already empty, with the staff beginning to set up the tables for breakfast the following day. She was glad it hadn't rained that evening, despite the pronounced humidity in the air and occasional streaks of lightning on the evening sky.

She watched as Royce took his infinite black credit card and replaced it in his wallet. She'd seen how much their bill was minutes ago; it had been eye-wateringly exorbitant. The tip Royce had added on was almost as much as their bill, but she knew better than to comment.

Instead, she focused on the warmth of the rich black coffee settling in her stomach; on the smile of the handsome, expensively dressed man with her. She could allow herself to pretend for a few more minutes, couldn't she? Pretend that she belonged in his world.

Before she could answer his question, the restaurant staff began to gather around their table, approaching Royce with smiles and murmured words of gratitude, most of them speaking on behalf of loved ones who had gotten jobs at Boundless Tower. The restaurant manager came over, too, and profusely apologized for the interruption, but Royce waved it off.

"It's okay, Joey. I'm happy to hear so many people have found jobs with Boundless. That's exactly the reason why we decided to set up our operations here."

She watched the exchange, both impressed and touched by the genuine respect and admiration the staff held for Royce.

As the employees dispersed, leaving them alone once more, she finally found her voice.

"No," she said, surprising even herself. "I don't want to go home yet. I want to go dancing in the club."

I don't want this night with you to end, she wanted to add. *Not yet.*

Royce raised an eyebrow, clearly surprised at her declaration. "Dancing, huh? We've never done any dancing in the past, have we?"

She shook her head. "You're not too old to try and find out who's better on the dance floor, are you, Mr. Duran?"

The challenge in her words was unmistakable. Oh, she still knew how to bait him.

His eyes widened in surprise, but he quickly recovered, a playful smirk tugging at the corner of his lips as he shook his head.

"I knew you're not the kind of man to back down," she teased.

"Very well, Miss Cisco." Royce stood up, offering her his arm. "Then what are we waiting for?"

The hotel club was a different world compared to the serene poolside restaurant. It pulsed with vibrant lights and thumping beats, the sheer energy of the place a welcome rush to Koreen's senses.

Royce guided her through the crowd of dancing bodies with a confident hand on her back, his body brushing against hers as they walked towards the bar. His warmth and the protective—almost possessive—way he moved made her giddy.

"Two glasses of red wine, please," he told the bartender, turning to her with a grin. "We'll need some liquid courage before hitting the dance floor. Or would you prefer something stronger?"

She shook her head and accepted the glass he handed her. "I didn't take you for the shy type, Duran."

"Trust me, I'm not," he replied, raising his glass in a toast. "To us."

She didn't question his meaning; instead, she settled onto the stool next to him, allowing her body to relax against the wooden countertop as she savored his warmth next to her.

As they sipped their wine, they reminisced about their shared childhood, laughing over stories of their intense rivalry at school, and how they had always tried to outdo the other in science fairs and quiz bees.

She was only too aware that, as the conversation went on, he began to touch her more casually, his hand brushing her arm or resting on the small of her back as he leaned in to speak. Each contact sent a thrill through her, making her heart race faster than she'd like to admit.

She began to relax into his touch and his presence, almost leaning against him by the time they finished their drinks. He welcomed it, seemingly, sliding his arm around her waist to hold her up and keep her close at the same time.

"You've been talking a big game all night, Mr. CEO," she said against his shoulder, feeling the world around her sway slightly. "Time to put your money where your mouth is. Let's dance."

"Challenge accepted, Sensei." The smile on his face was almost a sneer as he took her hand and led her onto the dance floor.

The music was fast, but he held her close, his hands firm on her waist. They swayed together, their bodies pressed tightly against one another as they tried to keep up with the beat.

"Sorry," Royce murmured in her ear. "I'm not much of a dancer. This is one thing I'm going to concede with no regrets."

Koreen laughed. "I can't dance to save my life, either. Give me all the hardest forms sequence of any martial art, any day."

"Nobody can beat you at any kata," he agreed with a grin, his arms around her tightening. "Not even me."

As the music pulsed around them, people swaying and twisting to the beat, he pulled her even closer, pressing their bodies together she could almost feel his body heat seeping into her, weaving its way through the barrier of their clothing. His cool, citrusy cologne, mixed with the light musky scent of his sweat, was intoxicating to her already overwhelmed senses.

She couldn't bring herself to deny that there was an electrifying connection between them, a magnetic pull she couldn't quite resist.

So she gave in, her hands settling on his chest, fingers digging into the fabric of his shirt, as she leaned against him and welcomed the thrum of his heartbeat against her ear. She sighed as she swayed against him, aware but not caring that their movements were out of sync with the rapid tempo of the music.

"Hey, are you okay?" He drew back and lifted her chin with a gentle hand. He looked sheepish and slightly uncertain, as if he didn't know what to say or do next. The change from his usual confident demeanor was surprisingly endearing.

"Must be the wine," she replied lightly, trying to deflect

her attraction onto something external. "So much for liquid courage."

They shared a moment of laughter, the tension between them disappearing for a few seconds. But the moment of levity was gone as quickly as it had come, replaced by a surge of desire that ignited every fiber of her body.

"Maybe we didn't need it," Royce said softly, his thumb tracing her lower lip, before his arms reached around her to pull her back in. "Maybe we had it in us all along."

Before she knew it, their lips met in a tentative, exploratory kiss. Koreen found herself surrendering to the passion that had been simmering beneath the surface all evening. The kiss deepened, growing more urgent and intense as she allowed herself to get lost in his arms.

She registered the fact that he'd lifted her off the floor, so smoothly and effortlessly. She marveled at his strength, even as her body instinctively responded to his touch.

"Can we go?" she gasped when they finally broke apart, her breath coming in short, uneven pants.

"Of course." His voice was strained and tight as he set her down gently, his hands lingering on her waist and venturing downward to trace the curve of her hips, as if he couldn't let her go completely.

Their eyes met, locking wordlessly. Her hand slipped into his, so naturally it felt like he'd always been meant to hold it. He brought her fingers to his lips and pressed a brief kiss to her knuckles.

With a nod from her, they turned to leave the dance floor, pausing only to grab her bag from the bar. Royce's grip was warm and firm was they walked out of the club.

Her steps were slightly unsteady from the mix of alcohol

and raw emotion coursing through her. She clung to him as he guided her to the elevators.

It was only when they were inside that she noticed that they were going up, not down towards the lobby.

He was taking her to his room.

Her heart pounded as they stepped out of the elevator and into the dimly lit hallway. She hesitated, swallowing hard as she let his hand go. "I know where we're going."

He paused mid-step and turned to face her, his eyes searching his face. "Hey, if you don't want this, it's okay. I'll take you home right now. I thought…well, I thought you wanted this as much as I do."

She stared in shock at his confession, her pulse quickening even more. "Is that why you asked me out? Because you wanted me?"

"Yes," he admitted without hesitation. "You're the reason I came back to town, the reason I wanted to build Boundless Tower here in Iloilo."

"What are you talking about, Duran?" The words escaped her even as her mind tried to process his previous answer.

"I've always admired your brilliance, Koreen." His voice was soft, tinged with what sounded like sadness and self-doubt. "I wanted to be someone worthy of you, when the time came that I could finally be with you."

"Be with…me?" The idea sent her reeling; it was a surprise that she was still on her feet, steady enough to remain standing.

He nodded. "I was hoping you'll give me a chance, but I'll understand if you don't want to. I'm sorry if I crossed any lines."

"You want to be with me? Is that what you're saying?"

His broad shoulders heaved in a sigh. "I'm surprised you haven't realized this."

She stood there, rooted to the spot, her world shifting beneath her feet. The intensity of his gaze made her feel exposed.

"I never knew." Her voice trembled as her mind struggled to up. "Why didn't you tell me before?"

He looked away for a moment, as if gathering his thoughts, before meeting her gaze once more. "I did, with that flower I gave you years ago. I needed you to understand that I've always wanted to be with you, no matter what you felt for me."

The memory of that single anemone surfaced in her mind; the petals wilting until she couldn't hold on to them any longer. As the flower fell apart, so did she. She could still remember the sleepless nights she'd cried over Royce Duran, cried over losing her chance at telling him how much he really meant to her.

Fifteen years later, the same person stood before her and, yet, she could only see her own uncertainties.

He spoke softly, his face unreadable in the sparse light of the corridor. "It took me weeks to find that single anemone, but I never gave up because I wanted you to have something special. If you'd asked me to stay back then, I probably would have found a way. You meant that much to me."

Tears began to fill her eyes, blurring her vision as she struggled to comprehend the enormity of what he was saying.

Royce wasn't finished, his voice becoming more unsteady as he went on. "When I left my belt with you all those years ago…it meant I left part of myself with you, too. I'd never be whole again until I was back with you. I wanted to tell you before I left, Koreen. Believe me, I did my best."

A strangled sob escaped her throat. "You're crazy! You're fucking crazy, and this doesn't make any sense."

His face contorted with exasperation, his hands balling into fists at his sides. "What the hell do you want me to say? How the fuck can I make you understand?"

"I don't know!" she cried, wiping angrily at her eyes. "I just—I have to go. I'll get a taxi."

She turned on her heel and sprinted down the hallway. She could feel his eyes on her as she fled to the elevators.

"Koreen, wait!" Royce called out, but she refused to look back.

As the elevator doors closed behind her, she leaned against the cold steel wall, her legs trembling beneath her as sobs racked her body.

But she refused to fall.

She stumbled into the hotel lobby, her heart sinking as she spied the heavy rain pouring outside, clearly visible through the windows and the glass doors of the main entrance.

Koreen blinked away tears and readjusted her bag on her shoulder, trying to regain her composure while approaching the front desk. A young woman with wire-rimmed glasses was manning reception at the late hour, tapping away at her computer.

"Excuse me, miss," she said in the clearest, strongest voice she could muster. "Could you please call me a taxi? I need to go home."

The receptionist looked up at her and glanced out the floor-to-ceiling windows of the lobby, concern furrowing her brow. "I'm afraid it might be difficult to find a taxi at this hour with the weather being so bad, ma'am. If you're willing to wait, I'll do my best."

Koreen nodded, then ventured further, remembering the sleek vehicle that had picked her up from the training center earlier. "What about the hire cars?"

She could only imagine how much they would cost, but, in her desperation, money was the least of her worries.

"They're based offsite, but I can try and get one for you in the morning as soon as their office opens."

A quick glance at the digital clock on the wall indicated it was almost midnight. Koreen sighed resignedly, forcing herself to bear up. "That's fine. I'll take whatever's available first."

"You came in with Mr. Duran, didn't you? Would you like for me to call his room, let him know you're down here?" The receptionist's gaze was mostly sympathetic, but there was a touch of curiosity in them as she mentioned Royce's name.

Koreen shook her head. "It's fine. I don't want to bother him. I'd be happy to wait right here."

"Of course, ma'am. Please let me know if you need anything. I'll try and make some calls for your taxi."

"Thank you." She turned away from the front desk and looked around the warm lobby, trying to figure out the best place to settle in for the night. With the way the rain pelted against the glass and the wind howled outside the thick walls of the hotel, the storm had made landfall in the time frame predicted.

She pulled out her phone from her bag, wincing when she saw there was no signal from her mobile network. The strong winds had probably knocked out the nearby tower.

She spotted a small balcony overlooking the city, sheltered

from the rain by a tile roof, and decided to try and get a signal from a better vantage point.

She stepped outside, feeling stray droplets of rain land on her arms and feet, soaking through her dress and shoes. No luck. The service bars on the screen remained hidden.

Koreen was about to return to the dry, welcoming lobby when Royce appeared beside her on the balcony.

The concern she saw in his eyes sent a sharp, stabbing sensation right through her chest. The last time she felt something close to it was at the football field all those years ago, when he'd asked her to let him know about her decision to compete in the nationals.

With Royce's departure from Iloilo, followed a few months later by her father's death, she'd withdrawn from the nationals and quit Karate. She'd then joined another club and tried to learn Sanda, another martial art. If not for Shihan Tuazon and his wife, who had visited her at home to offer her a part-time teaching job, she would never have returned to Karate.

"Please don't send me away, Koreen."

She could hear the defeat in his voice, as present-day Royce took a few tentative steps closer.

"I won't," she replied, her voice coming out hoarsely, from the cold and the stinging remnants of her tears. "I just want to leave. I'm tired."

"Fine, you can go whenever you want. I won't hold you back." He stepped directly into her line of sight, oblivious to the rain falling on his clothes and hair. "If you could just be honest with me about one thing, I'll leave you alone. I won't bother you again."

Curiosity mingled with her exhaustion as she looked up

into his unyielding eyes, inwardly telling herself that she could survive this moment, survive this night. "What is it?"

"Can you remember what you did with that flower I gave you? Did you throw it away? Please tell me."

Memories of the delicate anemone and the hidden emotions it represented flooded her mind. She opened her mouth to answer, but no words came out.

Royce sighed, his shoulders slumping as he accepted her silence as an answer.

"Of course you threw it away," he said quietly. "What else would you do, right?"

She looked away, unable to look at the pain clearly etched on his face. She felt the same pain inside, multiplied by a hundred. She was familiar with it; she felt it every single time she looked at their photo on the shelf.

"Look," he continued, taking a step back and glancing towards the interior of the hotel, "if you want to stay here tonight, I'll pay for a room for you. In the morning, I'll arrange for a car to take you home. It's the least I can do after all the trouble."

He paused, as if waiting for her reaction. After a few seconds without a response from her, he went on, in a much softer voice, "Goodbye, Koreen. I'm glad I got to see you again."

With that, he turned away from her and began to make his way back into the lobby.

"Royce."

His name escaped her lips, the sound almost foreign to her ears. She'd never called him by his first name before.

Only now. Because now was all she had.

"Wait," she called out, her voice cracking with emotion in that single word.

He heard her. She could see the tension in his back as he stopped just outside the balcony door.

Tears filled her eyes as the past bubbled and burst its way to the surface of her heart. "I never threw the flower away. I held it every night until it fell apart, and I kept the petals… with your belt. They were my memories of you. The only ones I could hold."

Her words hung heavy in the air between them. Time seemed to slow, too, as the years and the rain-drenched world faded away and she could see only him, right there in front of her.

Slowly, he turned to face her once more.

"Say my name again. Please."

She knew, then, that everything had changed.

"Royce," she repeated.

Without another thought, she rushed towards him, her heels echoing loudly against the rain-slicked tiles of the balcony.

She threw herself into his embrace, seeking solace in the strength she'd always admired. He caught her effortlessly.

"Royce," she said once more, before her lips crashed against his, with a desperate passion that put the raging storm to shame.

EIGHT

Royce

REVELATION

THE FORCE OF HER CONFESSION HIT HIM LIKE A TIDAL wave.

She'd kept it.

All these years, she'd kept it with her.

Disbelief washed over him as his world tilted on its axis, leaving him breathless.

"Koreen."

Her name was swallowed by the rain, the howling wind.

It didn't matter.

Instead, he asked her to repeat his.

So she did.

The sound fell on his ears like a gentle caress. He had never been 'Royce' to her. He'd only ever been 'Duran.'

Before he could even comprehend what was happening, she sprinted across the balcony, her hair whipping wildly. She hurled herself into his arms, and suddenly, everything felt right.

Royce could scarcely feel his own muscles as they instinctively moved to catch her. She fit into his arms perfectly, as though he was always meant to hold her, protect her, *love* her.

She said his name again, both a plea and a command, and he obliged. Their lips met and they were kissing hungrily, years of pent-up emotion crammed into a single act.

Her body trembled against his as she clung to him tightly. She pulled back to speak, her breath warm against his cheek, in a broken whisper. "I never knew. I never understood…I thought I'd never see you or touch you again."

Her sobs tore at his heart, and for the first time, he saw her vulnerability beneath the fierce exterior. A wisp of a woman, heartbreakingly beautiful, smart, and strong, held together by the sheer force of her own will.

He could feel the urgency in her grasp, the longing in her voice. This was the first time he had seen her lose control. He pulled her closer; she could fall apart and he would be with her every step of the way.

"I'm here, Koreen," he murmured into her hair. "I'll never leave you again."

"This is real, isn't it?" she sobbed against his shoulder, her tears soaking through the material of his shirt.

"More real than anything I've ever known," he replied, his lips brushing against her forehead tenderly.

"This isn't even possible…" she breathed.

He could feel her trembling in his embrace, so he lifted her off the ground, unwilling to let her slip away from him again. "Do you want me to kiss you again, like in the club? Just to make sure this is all real?"

She nodded slowly, her eyes never leaving his face. "Yes."

His heart skipped a beat at her agreement. He'd fantasized about this moment for years. And now, here she was, their lips just inches apart. He leaned in, their mouths meeting in a fiery kiss that stole the air from his lungs.

He felt her arms wrap tightly around his neck, her legs encircling his hips, closing the space between them. Through her tears and their veil of raindrops, she kissed him back with reckless abandon.

He slid his tongue into her mouth, tasting her sweetness—a flavor he had never imagined possible. As their tongues danced together, he tightened his hold on her, his hands tangling in her hair.

She welcomed his touch, her hands fisting in his shirt. The kiss was raw and powerful, untamed and unrestrained.

As they parted, breathless and panting, he realized this was what he had been missing; the taste of her on his tongue, the feel of her softness against his hardness.

"Do you still want me?" Her question was tentative, her voice quivering with the cold and something else, something undeniable that bound them to each other.

"More than anything." His answer, in contrast, left no room for doubt or argument. "I've always wanted you. Ever since we were children, ever since I understood what a boy could feel for a girl."

Her eyes widened. "But I thought you never saw me as a girl, only as someone who just one-upped you at every turn."

He laughed, planting tender kisses along her jawline. "You're the most beautiful woman in the world to me, Koreen.

I've seen so many people, but none of them could ever compare to you. Nobody could ever outshine you."

As they kissed again, Royce felt her body rubbing against him passionately. He was already painfully aroused, and he couldn't keep his distance any longer. His body burned for hers. "Would it be okay if you stayed with me, Koreen? Just… be with me."

She nodded eagerly, her eyes glistening as she reached up to touch his cheek. "I want to be with you, too. More than anything."

He smiled at the way she echoed his earlier admission and carefully set her back down on the rain-soaked balcony, straightening their disheveled clothes before placing a protective arm around her.

He led her across the lobby and to the front desk. The receptionist looked up as they approached, an apologetic smile on her face.

"I'm really sorry, ma'am," she said to Koreen. "I tried calling a taxi for you, but none of them could get through the city. It's starting to flood outside."

"Miss Cisco won't be needing the taxi after all, Stephanie," Royce said. "She'll be staying the night as my guest."

The receptionist nodded. "Very well, Mr. Duran. I'll make a note on your booking."

"Could you please call Mrs. Cisco and let her know that her daughter will be spending the night at the hotel? It's best for her safety. I'll ensure everything is taken care of."

"Of course, sir. Can I have Mrs. Cisco's number?"

Koreen hesitated only briefly before providing her mother's number. As they left the reception area, they found themselves hidden from sight, waiting for the elevator. The momentary privacy provided them with an opportunity to resume their passionate kissing.

His hands cupped her face as he whispered between kisses, "Do you want this, Koreen? I could always book a separate room for you if you'd rather."

Shaking her head, she touched his face again, her fingers tracing the contours of his lips.

"No," she said, almost shyly, a pink flush staining her cheeks. "I want to be with you. And...I've always wanted this."

A warm smile spread across his face as they stepped into the elevator. He kept her close to him and pressed soft kisses to her hair, never letting her go as they ascended to the penthouse.

Once they were in the hallway, he swept her off her feet and into his arms as they made their way to his suite. Fumbling slightly with the key card, he was rewarded by the sound of her giggles and the sensation of her lips brushing against his jaw and neck.

"I really like you with a beard," she murmured, her breath warm against his skin. "You look like a very rich sheikh or something."

He chuckled at her comment, finally managing to unlock the door and step inside. He immediately switched on the 'Do Not Disturb' sign before carrying her to the bedroom and gently laying her down on the bed.

"I'm done controlling myself around you, Koreen."

He didn't know if it was meant to be a precaution or a promise, but it was the truth. She needed to hear it.

"I don't want to hold back anymore either," she replied softly, her fingers playing with the hem of his shirt. "We've already wasted so much time."

He reached out to caress her face. "I agree. Let's not waste any more."

He lowered his lips to hers, initiating a tender kiss that quickly grew more passionate. His hands moved down her body, deftly unzipping her dress and sliding it off her shoulders and arms. The shimmering fabric pooled around her waist, revealing a black strapless bra.

"You're so beautiful, Sensei," he whispered against her skin as he trailed kisses down her neck, nibbling at the soft flesh.

The scent of her perfume and the sweet taste of her skin reminded him of strawberries. He could feel her pulse quickening beneath his lips.

He reached behind her and unclasped her bra, pulling it away to reveal full, round breasts. He stared at them in wonder, unable to believe that someone so petite could have such perfect proportions. His fingers traced the curve of her breasts before his mouth followed suit, licking and sucking at her nipples until they were pebble-hard.

As he continued to worship her breasts with his mouth, his hand snaked its way down her body and between her legs. To his delight, she was wet and ready through her panties. Using the pad of his thumb, he began to rub her in slow circles, matching the rhythm of his mouth on her nipples. Her moans grew louder, her fingers digging into his back as she writhed beneath him.

"Tell me," he whispered, drawing back for a moment. "Have you always been mine?"

"I've always wanted to be yours," she replied, her eyes dark pools of desire in the dim light of the room. "But there were…others."

"Others?" he echoed, reaching around the cover of her damp underwear and sliding a finger into her slit, eliciting a squeal.

"Other men," she gasped out. "Two…a long time ago."

"Tell me about them," he urged gently, inserting another finger into her and increasing the tempo of his ministrations on her nipples.

Panting, she ground against his hand as she spoke, her breasts bouncing on his face. "One was a PE teacher I met at a tournament. We broke up after six months…and he left town. The other was a Korean Taekwondo instructor…he was a fling during a martial arts conference in Manila. This was…oh…years ago."

White-hot jealousy coursed through him at the idea of those unknown men seeing her naked, touching her, *having her*. A low, almost angry growl escaped his throat as he increased the pace of his fingers inside her. "Did either of them ever make you feel like this?"

"No, never like this," she managed, her body tensing. Her hips lifted off the bed, as if reaching for something more.

"Are you sure?" he asked softly, sliding up to give her a feather-light kiss on the lips. He slid his other arm under her and raised her torso off the pillows. "What about this?"

Without warning, he slid his tongue into her mouth, just as he redoubled his efforts between her legs.

The feeling of her draped over his arm was almost too much. Her long hair, soft and damp, tickled his skin. Her bare breasts were crushed against his chest. Her mouth was hot, her core even hotter. There was nothing more he wanted to do than tear off her dress and take her.

But he'd waited fifteen years; he could wait fifteen seconds more.

Koreen was moaning incoherently against him, into his mouth, clutching his arms for dear life.

He knew she was almost there, at the very edge. He slowed the pace of his fingers, causing her to groan in protest. He slanted his lips against hers before he spoke again. "And what about this, Koreen?"

He'd had his fair share of women, but he'd never felt the need for affirmation as he did with her now. He should have been her first, he thought with a twinge of regret and self-loathing. They should have been each other's first—and last.

She was panting, both in urgency and frustration, but he knew her pride would keep her talking.

"Only you, Royce," she whispered into his neck. "Only you."

Satisfaction coursed through him at her admission. "Good. Now let's begin."

He pulled the last of Koreen's dress away and slowly rolled her panties down her legs, kissing the path of the silken fabric as it brushed against her skin. She squirmed as he did; he wasn't sure if she was ticklish or highly aroused. He would like it very much if she were both.

With Koreen now completely naked before him, he wrapped his arms around her and kissed her soundly.

"My queen," he said against her lips. "You're mine now. You'll only ever be mine."

"Always yours, Royce," she whispered, her breath sweet and warm on his cheek.

He kissed her deeply once more before settling her back down on the pillows.

"Now, open wide for me," he commanded, his voice hoarse with need.

With her eyes never leaving his, she obediently spread her legs, revealing the glistening curls at the apex of her thighs.

"Wider," he said, and she complied, baring herself completely to him.

The sight of her like this—open, waiting, wanting—was almost too much for him. He wanted to do nothing else but devour her, every sweet inch of her, but he knew he needed to take his time.

He lowered himself between her legs, bringing his hungry mouth to her sensitive flesh. He began slowly, teasing her with his lips and tongue, making her buck beneath him.

"Royce," she whimpered, her hands gripping the sheets.

"Tell me what you want, Koreen," he murmured, his mouth an inch away from her wet, heated core. The sound of his name on her lips made his pants feel tighter. He was now very, very hard.

"Your mouth, your tongue…all of it," she panted, grinding against his mouth as if there was no tomorrow.

"Can you take it?"

"I…"

Before she could answer, he began to increase his pace. He explored every inch of her, using his hands, lips, and tongue. Her moans grew louder as he brought her closer and closer to release.

"I can't… I'm going to…" she gasped, her legs trembling on his shoulders as her hips ground against his mouth. With her head lolling back and her hair spread on his pillow, her lips parted and her face tight as she sought her own pleasure, he'd never seen anything more beautifully erotic.

"Let go, Koreen," he urged, his fingers digging into her thighs as he lapped at her like a starving man. "Give yourself to me."

With a strangled cry, she shattered in his arms, her body shaking with the force of her climax. He drank her in greedily, savoring every last drop.

As he waited for her to come down from the high of her orgasm, he slid up next to her and cradled her in arms, pressing gentle kisses to her hair and cheeks. He could still taste her on his lips, making it difficult for him to think about anything else other than how much he wanted to be inside her.

He didn't have to wait very long.

As soon as she got her bearings and breath back, Koreen grabbed him by the collar, pressing her naked body against his own fully clothed one.

"Kiss me," she demanded, her eyes gleaming in the dim lamplight.

He obliged, his lips capturing hers in a searing kiss. As they broke apart, she shifted her position in a perfectly executed mount, straddling him and grinding her heat against his rock-hard arousal.

"My turn." Her voice was soft, but her fingers were steady and urgent as she began to unbutton his shirt. Once his chest was exposed, she dove in, licking and nibbling at his pecs and nipples.

"Fuck, Koreen…" His fingers tangled in her hair as a groan escaped his throat. The sensation of her warm mouth and teeth on his flesh was maddening.

"Be a good boy, Duran," she murmured against his chest. "You need to warm up properly."

He wasn't warm; he was on fire. He gritted his teeth as her hands wandered south, from his chest to his stomach.

She unbuckled his belt slowly and slithered her way down until she was between his legs. "Have you ever imagined me doing this to you?"

"Fuck, yeah," he bit out, his body tensing in anticipation.

She slid his slacks and underwear just low enough to free his arousal from its confines. She raised an eyebrow at the sight of him. "And what about this?"

The way she'd asked the same question as he had earlier only served to make him even harder. She took his cock in her hands and brought it to her lips, her tongue swirling at the tip as she cupped his balls and squeezed delicately.

"God, yes," he gasped, unable to contain himself as his hips bucked in response. "All the time."

"Really?"

Before he could utter a coherent answer, she took him into her mouth, sliding the whole of him in and out between her lips.

"Fuck, Koreen…" He had no words except for these two, as pleasure built rapidly from within him.

She knew exactly what she was doing, and she was doing it so damn well. He held on to her hair as her mouth increased its pace; silken locks fell around her face and brushed against his skin, compounding the assault on his senses.

Before Royce knew it, he was tipping over the edge, his body wracked with an intense climax. With a muffled moan, she swallowed every last drop from him, her eyes meeting his with challenge and satisfaction. He watched hazily as she got up and pulled off his pants and socks.

"My queen," he called out, his voice hoarse in the aftermath of his explosive orgasm.

She smiled, her tongue flicking out to lick her bottom lip as she went on her hands and knees. This was the first time he fully understood what the phrase 'the cat that swallowed the canary' meant. "Yes?"

"Come here," he rasped, holding out his arms.

She crawled to him until she was splayed over his much larger frame like a blanket, the weight of her settling across him deliciously. The sight of her full breasts in front of his face was enough to make him go hard again.

"I like this. You're like a very hot beanbag, literally and figuratively. With a beard." She giggled, her tongue flicking out to trace the facial hair on his jawline.

"I like this, too."

She nuzzled his neck. "Can I ask you something?"

"Anything," he replied, his hands exploring her back, lowering to cup her toned backside.

"Are you…really single? Do you have a girlfriend? A fiancée? A wife waiting for you back in Saudi?"

He laughed. "No, I don't have any of those. I had a girlfriend in college, but it barely lasted a year. My only serious relationship was about seven years ago; she was a Serbian air hostess. We started out great, but she wanted a rich man to fund her lifestyle…and I've only ever wanted one person all along. Apparently, she's now the second wife of some Bahraini financier." He shook his head slightly at the memory of Yulia, glamorous and demanding, who could never seem to quash the memory of the woman now in his arms. "Since then, I haven't had any relationships. My schedule barely gives me any free time."

"And this one person you wanted all along…?"

"She's with me now. Right here."

He heard her take a deep breath against his shoulder. He tightened his arms around her in response.

"No one could really quite live up to you, even when you're so far away." Her voice was almost swallowed by the muffled sound of rain. "I always end up comparing every guy with you…and no one even comes close."

The honesty he had always admired now tugged at his heartstrings, refusing to let go. "I guess that settles it, then."

"Settles what?"

"That you've always been mine, Koreen."

She brushed her lips against his in a feather-light kiss. "I guess there's only one thing left to do, then."

"What's that?"

"Isn't it obvious?" Her voice lowered to a sultry whisper. "You should take what's always been yours."

He immediately understood what she wanted, what she needed. He kissed her back before flipping her over, pinning her beneath him.

He'd never been this aroused in his life, never felt such a primal, insatiable need for another person before. It was all-consuming, and he knew he would never be sated.

"I should, shouldn't I?"

She nodded, her eyes never leaving his.

He pinned her arms above her head, lacing their fingers together as he slid his length along her slick folds. Their eyes locked, and he could see his raw hunger mirrored in her eyes as he began to push inside her. She gasped, her teeth sinking into his shoulder, her grip on his hands tightening until he thought his bones might break.

"Mine," he said into her hair, filling her completely in one thrust. Her mouth met his passionately, tongues tangling, as he started to move inside her, his hips snapping against hers with a force that made the bed creak beneath them.

She met each of his thrusts with equal fervor. The sounds of their moans and heavy breathing filled the room, punctuated by the distant rumble of thunder outside.

"Royce," she gasped, her back arching. "Don't stop… please, don't ever fucking stop."

He couldn't have stopped even if he'd wanted to, not with his name on her lips like that. The world seemed to narrow down to just the two of them, their bodies locked together in a dance of desire.

"Koreen," he groaned, feeling his own climax building like a storm within him. He could no longer hold back, and with one final thrust, he came with a shuddering cry, collapsing on top of her.

For several moments, they lay there, panting, his heart pounding loudly against hers. Their lips met, and he kissed her feverishly.

"Again," he murmured, feeling the fire within him reignite with alarming speed.

"Yes."

That was the only thing he needed to hear. He lifted her legs, folding her knees to her chest as he slid into her again, the new angle eliciting a whimper of delight and surprise. They moved together in perfect harmony, until they were both trembling from an earth-shattering release once more.

He took her from behind next, as he stood by the edge

of the bed, his thrusts going deeply into her as she went up on her hands and knees, her backside his for the taking. The sight of himself driving into her butt almost made him pass out from the pleasure that followed.

But they weren't done—not even close.

She pushed him back onto the bed and straddled him with a wicked grin. She moved with the confidence of a goddess, her hips undulating and bouncing in perfectly timed movements that drove him to the brink of insanity. He fondled her breasts and tweaked her clit, coaxing wave after wave of pleasure from her body, and she finally gave in, taking him to the peak with her.

With a cry that seemingly echoed throughout the hotel, she finally collapsed on top of him, whimpering and shaking.

"Always mine," he said as he pulled her close, not even sure if she heard him.

"Yours, Royce," she answered shakily, her eyes fluttering shut as she curled into his body as if she had always belonged there.

Entwined in each other's arms, they both drifted off to sleep.

Habit made him open his eyes even before first light. His body had learned to adjust to his routine, and he demanded nothing less from it.

The lights flickering outside the bedroom window showed it was still dark. The heavy rain displayed no signs of abating; the sound now an almost soothing staccato he was getting accustomed to.

The dim orange lamplight cast a gentle glow on Koreen's face as she slept in his arms. The sheer sight took Royce aback. He watched her with wonder, unable to shake off the feeling that this was all just a dream and any moment he would wake up alone. But as her chest rose and fell with each breath, he knew that this was real—she was right there, and she was his.

As if sensing his gaze, she stirred, her eyes slowly drifting open. She looked up at him with a sleepy smile.

"Hi." He smiled back and kissed her on the forehead, inhaling her light strawberry-like scent, now mingled with their night of passion.

"Hi." Her voice was husky as she reached up to trace her fingertips along his jawline.

His body responded to her touch, desire already stirring within him.

"Shower?" he suggested.

"Yes, please."

With a grin, he scooped her up into his arms and carried her to the bathroom. As water cascaded over their bodies, they couldn't keep their hands off each other, fingers exploring every inch of bare skin they could touch.

She pressed herself against him, her breasts rubbing against his chest as she reached up to pull him into a kiss. Their mouths moved together hungrily as the water streamed down around them.

Unable to wait a second more, he picked her up, her legs wrapping around his waist as he pushed himself inside her, their lovemaking taking on a new urgency beneath the spray of the shower.

Later, still damp and flushed, they tumbled onto the plush

carpet of the living area, the full-length windows offering a view of the dark, stormy skyline of the city.

He laid down on the floor and pulled her to him, whispering a request in her ear that made her laugh and blush. She relented without hesitation and, before long, she was on top of him, her wondrous mouth moving up and down his length, as he licked, sucked and fingered her from a new, tantalizing vantage point.

She wanted something, too, but it was more of a demand. She pushed him down onto the plush beige couch and guided his length inside her once more. It was a different angle; her breasts pushed against his face, her clit rubbing against his pelvis.

In a pleasure-induced high, he watched her ride him with wild abandon, his hands reaching up to cup her breasts and thumb her nipples. The sensations were overwhelming, pleasure building within him like a tidal wave.

"Move with me, Royce," she panted. "I can't get enough of you."

"Neither can I," he admitted, his hands gripping her hips as he thrust up into her, their bodies meeting and, finally, coming together.

Once he got feeling back in his legs, he carried her to the bed and slid in next to her, pulling the thick comforter over their exhausted bodies.

But Koreen Cisco always knew how to one-up everything. As they lay there, spooned together, she shifted, grinding her backside against him. He heard a groan of desire escape his lips in response to her invitation.

He reached around to finger her soaked core once more. Once she was ready, he entered her from behind, lifting her leg to allow himself deeper access, and began to caress her clit as they moved together.

The pleasure they reached left them both breathless and, for the time being, spent. As she succumbed to sleep, her soft snores filling the room, Royce held her tightly, his fingers combing through her hair, his lips raining kisses on her skin, even as he felt sleep claim him, too.

His last thought was that, yes, she'd always belonged with him.

NINE

Koreen

RESONANCE

She stirred from her slumber, heavy warmth enveloping her like a blanket. As the haze of sleep lifted, she realized it was Royce's arms around her, his snores somehow a rhythmic, comforting sound to her ears.

In the thin morning light that seeped through the slightly open electronic blinds, Koreen took in the sight of the man who held her so tenderly—his short dark hair, chiseled jawline covered with a hint of beard, and his muscular frame that was equally intimidating and reassuring.

The rain and wind still raged outside, but nothing could dampen the heat that fluttered in her chest as memories of the previous night surfaced. It had been incredible, so much better than anything she'd ever dared imagine; his body entwined with hers, his desire for and power over her overwhelming. She felt a blush creep up her cheeks as arousal stirred within her at the thought of all the delicious things they did to each other.

As she traced her fingers lightly over the contours of his face, now sharpened and hardened by time, she realized this was her first time waking up in a man's arms.

In Royce Duran's arms, of all people.

His eyes fluttered open, and he looked at her with a drowsy frown. "Don't wake me up, Koreen. I don't want you to go."

"Who said I'm going anywhere?" she replied softly, wrapping her arms around his neck and snuggling closer.

He pulled her tighter against his chest, the beat of his heart a steady rhythm in her ear. No sooner had she settled comfortably did she realize he was asleep again.

He'd always been steady and strong, ever since they were children. Tears prickled unbidden at the corners of her eyes as she thought of how many times she'd wanted to have him with her, only to realize that he was gone from her life.

For a moment, she gave in to the indulgence of ignoring the storm-drenched city outside their own little world, focusing only on the feeling of his skin against hers, the scent of him mixed with soap and their passion.

Later can wait, she decided, her fingers dancing lightly over the curve of his shoulder and down his arm.

The world can wait.

For now, she had Royce, and that was enough.

As she lay in the protective cocoon of his embrace, afloat

between sleep and waking, memories of their shared past began to surface.

There was a time when they were both eleven years old, when her unnamed feelings for him had first taken root.

She had been training tirelessly for an upcoming regional junior kata competition; she'd worked hard for two years just to qualify and make it through the city-wide and provincial rounds. Her life at that time was filled with challenges—her brother Kenneth was in the hospital, very sick from dengue fever, while her mother stayed by his side and her father scrambled to gather enough money for his medication. Koreen was left to navigate the world alone, commuting to and from the gym each day.

One evening, after an especially grueling training session, Royce had found her huddled in a corner of the gym as they waited for a special technique class with their school's Shihan, Mr. Tuazon. He'd pulled out a sandwich and a packet of juice from his bag, offering both to her without hesitation.

Hunger had made her swallow her pride back then; she'd taken the food with a soft word of thanks and immediately started eating, to appease the angry monster gnawing at her insides.

"How are you getting home tonight?" He'd sat beside her, mimicking her huddled position a little awkwardly. His limbs had started growing and filling out; he looked less like a boy and more like a young man.

"I'm going to commute," she'd replied between bites of ham sandwich, trying to sound nonchalant, as if she was completely fine being on her own.

After training, Royce had insisted on making sure she got home safely. That night, he walked her to the jeepney stop, a different one from his own. Along the way, they came across a fishball vendor. Royce had ended up buying out the entire cart, as they both devoured the street food, with all its different sauces, until they were bursting.

She'd wanted to ask him how he knew about her struggles, but something had stopped her—her willingness not to admit that she was exhausted from running around on her own, perhaps, or that his help was more than appreciated.

His help was needed, and she'd never even asked.

Just before they parted ways, he'd pressed a twenty-peso bill into her hand without a word. By the time she realized he'd given her money, the jeepney she was on had already driven off, leaving him standing on the pavement.

It was in that moment, watching him from a distance as the night swallowed his lanky frame, Koreen realized how special Royce truly was.

The nightly walks to the jeepney stop became their silent, unofficial ritual for two weeks, until the kata competition came and went. As she stood beside him to have their picture taken, silver medals hanging proudly from around their necks, Koreen had wanted to say thank you, but the words never came.

They never did, not in the way she wanted to say them.

Back in the present, nestled in his arms, she felt warmth spread through her chest as the memory played out in her mind. How strangely and deeply their lives had intertwined back then—and how intense their connection had become now.

She allowed her eyes to open and settle on his sleeping form next to her. Still overwhelmed by the depth of emotion welling up inside her, she leaned in and pressed her lips to his, wanting to convey what she still couldn't find the courage to say.

Thank you for everything.

You have no idea how much I missed you.

A sole tear rolled down her cheek, as she thought of the most important thing she wanted him to tell him, but never could.

I've loved you for the longest time.

Koreen didn't realize she had fallen asleep watching him. As she once more stirred to wakefulness, she felt his gaze on her.

She found herself looking into his dark eyes, their depths still hazy with sleep. A smile tugged at the corner of his lips, and she couldn't resist leaning in to capture it with a lingering kiss.

Royce gave an appreciative moan. "This is the best way to wake up."

Kissing him with increased fervor, she felt her body respond to his touch as if it were the most natural thing in the world. Unable to help herself, she straddled him and she took his length into her body, the sensation of being filled by him exhilarating.

She rode him hard then, his hands gripping her hips tightly, guiding her movements as she brought him to the brink.

When she could no longer hold back, she surrendered herself to the waves of pleasure that crashed over them and promptly collapsed onto his chest.

"Good morning, my queen," he greeted her softly, brushing a strand of damp hair away from her face.

"Good morning," she replied, still breathless from their passionate encounter.

They lay in silence for several long moments, listening to the sound of the rain outside and their own breaths.

She was the first to speak. "Royce?"

His hands were idly twirling locks of her hair. "Yeah?"

"You told me you didn't have time for a relationship," she ventured. "But you're here with me…and you seem to have time. You asked for me at the gym, saw me at school, took me to dinner…" Her voice trailed off; she didn't want to appear assuming, or give herself any hope.

"This is my last shot with you, Koreen," he answered without hesitation. "I couldn't let you slip away from me without trying to be with you. As you said, we've already wasted so much time."

Her eyes stung as his words sunk in. "Why did you wait so long?"

His hands found her waist and, before she knew it, she was back in his arms, the warm comforter thrown over both their naked bodies.

Royce didn't speak at first, but continued his caresses, his fingers feather-light as they stroked her hair and skin.

"I wanted to make sure I could give you everything you've ever wanted," he finally said. "You're the only person who's ever made me feel like this…the only one I'd do anything and everything for. I never felt that with anyone else, only with you."

She closed her eyes, letting his words wash over her.

"Koreen..." His fingers were on her chin. "Please look at me."

She did, afraid of what she knew she would see. Afraid that, if she looked, she would be forever lost.

"Before I left, my boss, the owner of Boundless, told me something I've never even considered before. After I saw you, I realized he was right, all along."

"Right about what?" Confusion joined the myriad emotions already churning within her.

"Maybe you should consider getting married to me. I can't imagine being with anyone else. Being married to you would be heaven. Don't you think it would be heaven if we were married?"

She froze, her body rigid with shock. *Get married?* The thought had never crossed her mind before, but now it hung heavy in the air between them.

Swallowing hard, she grabbed a pillow and hugged it to her body, as if to shield herself from the immensity of what he was offering and the decision that lay before her.

Royce didn't miss a beat; as they lay side by side, he spoke passionately about how perfect they were for each other, how they complemented and fired each other up, and how together they were invincible. As he talked, his voice both soothing and persuasive, she found herself torn between wanting to give in to the idea and resisting the urge to succumb to something unknown, something beyond her control.

When he finished speaking, Royce reached out and caressed her cheek. She found herself weakening at the adoration in his eyes. "Look at you. My perfect warrior queen."

She reached up and caught his hand, feeling the warmth

of his skin and the steady pulse beneath. With a smile, she pressed her lips to his fingertips.

Still aching with longing for him, she slipped out of bed and wrapped herself in a robe she'd found in the closet last night but never got to use. She didn't need it then. She had the comfort of Royce's embrace.

She approached the glass windows of the bedroom and used the control to open the electronic blinds, revealing the gray, flooded cityscape below.

Numbly, she stared out at the dark, brooding sky. For the first time since she'd stepped into his suite, she felt cold, even underneath the thick, fluffy white robe.

Marriage.

Royce's wife.

Spending every night in his arms, building a life together. As beautiful and tantalizing as it sounded, she couldn't shake the feeling that it was all part of his plans, not hers.

Everything had been his plan.

As if sensing her unease, she heard Royce get out of bed.

"Hey." She felt the warmth of his voice in her ear, the heat of his naked body against hers. He wrapped his arms around her from behind, resting his chin on her shoulder. "Are you hungry?"

"Yes, I'm starving." She met his eyes in the glass, forcing a smile.

The sincere smile she got in response lit up his face. "Me, too. Let's get some breakfast. Or lunch. I'm not even sure what time it is."

As he spoke, she could feel his arousal pressing against her. His hand gradually found its way under the robe, slowly reaching for her breasts and heat as he used his other arm to pin her against his body. Each touch ignited a fire within her, making her wet, her nipples hardening under his touch.

"Royce…" she breathed, torn between the desire coursing through her and the weight of her own uncertainties.

"Be my wife, Koreen," he whispered against her neck, undoing her robe and letting it fall to the floor. He turned her around and effortlessly lifted her into his arms.

"Marry me." He entered her slowly, guiding her to sink into him. "Together we can do anything. You know that."

Koreen had no answer. Instead, she wrapped her arms around his neck, her legs encircling his hips. Their bodies entwined perfectly, echoes of the previous night on the balcony when they had first kissed. She lost herself in the heat of the moment, moving along with him fervently, desperately. Their lips met again and again, tongues tangling and breaths mingling.

He pushed her against the cold glass, the contrast between the chill and his warmth more pronounced as he drove into her with an intensity that left her gasping for air. She matched him stroke for stroke, climbing higher, needing to have all of him, before she had to let go.

"Koreen," he groaned, his grip tightening on her waist. She knew he was close; so she kissed him, hard, feeling tears rise to her eyes as she ground herself harder against him.

She knew it, then, as she gave her body to him, so willingly, holding nothing back.

She had always been his.

She reached the peak with a shudder that weakened her limbs, just as she felt him tense up within her, thrusting almost feverishly as he came. She held on tightly, her lips tasting the salt of his sweat as she buried her face into his neck, nibbling at his skin.

As their breathing slowly returned to normal, she disentangled herself from his embrace and pushed him to the floor.

On her hands and knees, she focused on the storm still raging outside the window.

"Again," she whispered, knowing he would rise to the challenge.

Never one to back down, Royce sank to his knees behind her. She moaned when she felt his lips and tongue lap at her dripping core before entering her from behind. His body covered hers, one hand grabbing her hair while the other firmly squeezed and pinched her breasts. He nipped and kissed the back of her neck and shoulder as he took her again, fiercely, mercilessly. She felt herself teetering on the edge, ready to shatter into a million pieces.

He went faster and harder, his hand moving to rub roughly against her clit. His voice was a growl in her ear as he said once more, "Marry me, Koreen."

She didn't respond; instead, she allowed herself and her heart to break.

He followed her, his breath hitching, his body convulsing above her with the force of his own release.

Together, they collapsed on the floor, Koreen face down and Royce sprawled atop her, still partially within her. She bore his weight without complaint, reveling in the feeling of him hot and pulsating inside her.

"You're mine, aren't you?" His voice was raw, almost vulnerable.

"Always."

Royce slowly brought himself up to a seated position. He pulled her up with him, his hands firm on her hips.

She climbed onto his lap, and their eyes met. So many questions and no sure answers.

If this were a Mathematics test, it would be a dismal failure, she thought darkly.

She embraced him, her lips finding his. She willed him not to say anything and ruin the moment.

But he did.

"Will you marry me, Koreen?"

The words were hopelessly fragile, ready to shatter under the weight of her answer.

Despite all her self-control, a lone tear slid down her cheek, cutting a path through the sheen of their mingled sweat on her skin.

It was a question that resonated with all the dreams she'd locked away in her heart for so long. But something held her back, something decidedly stronger.

Her answer was tremulous, broken, but ready.

"No."

TEN

Royce

RESTRAINT

It wasn't a sensation of tripping or falling—or even crashing.

It was *nothing*; the absence of everything. A blank numbness that closed in from around him. There was no more tension or emotion.

There was only emptiness, as the life he'd imagined for so long was seemingly ravaged and washed away by the storm outside.

But he still held on to her; his body was still fighting, unable to let go. "Why? Why won't you marry me?"

At least she still looked at him straight in the eye, her own gaze filled with something akin to sorrow. "I'm sorry. I can't keep up. This is all too much, too fast."

His arms tightened around her.

Please, don't, he wanted to say it so desperately, repeatedly, until she succumbed.

A lifetime of competition, of striving to be better than one another, had led them here. He had dedicated years to proving himself worthy of her, to becoming the man who could stand beside her as an equal. And now she was slipping through his fingers like sand.

"Koreen, aren't we meant to be equals?" he said instead. "To complete each other?"

She shook her head, her hair falling across her face. "You've always been the better half. You've always been the one looking out for me, giving all of yourself. I...I have nothing to give."

Their lips met in a desperate, searing kiss, and for a moment, time stood still. But then, with a quiet sob, she began to untangle herself from his embrace.

"That's not true," he insisted, grasping for any lifeline that might bring her back to him. "I don't want anything from you. Just you. You're all I've ever wanted."

She didn't respond, and as she stepped out of his arms, Royce felt the chasm between them widen, the wall between them rise and reinforce itself a hundredfold.

He could only stare as she moved around the room, the stillness between them heavy and oppressive. She avoided his gaze as she began to gather her scattered clothes. With each piece she collected, his own heart twisted more and more painfully in his chest.

To distract himself, he awkwardly stood up from the floor and picked out fresh clothes from the closet. The sound of her sipping water filled the room as he dressed quickly, feeling the weight of their unspoken words suffocating him. She was seated on the bed, rummaging through her bag.

He watched as she pulled out a comb and ran it through her hair. The simple act seemed to hold so much more meaning now. He felt a sudden urge to reach out to her, to close the distance that had formed between them.

"Do you want to eat something?" His voice broke the silence. It was the voice of a stranger.

"Yes." Her eyes met his for the first time since she'd stepped away from him. "If you could arrange for a car to take me home after, that would be great."

For a fleeting second, he entertained the thought of ordering in, of keeping her in the room with him, making love to her again and again. But instead, he nodded and reached for the phone.

"Good afternoon."

"Good afternoon, Mr. Duran." It was a different receptionist from last night.

"I'd like to book a table at the restaurant for lunch, please, and request a car to pick up Miss Cisco at three this afternoon."

"I'm really sorry, sir." The voice at the other end was deeply apologetic. "The storm is still at Signal Number Three. The streets are flooded, and no cars could get through the roads."

He glanced out the window, watching the rain and wind still whipping through the city mercilessly. Everything in his sight seemed doused with a bleak gray color.

"It's okay. We'll have lunch, anyway. Please let me know if any transport will be available."

"I will, Mr. Duran. Thank you for your understanding."

He hung up the phone, resisting the urge to bring his fist down on it. Why was everything fucked up, all of a sudden?

"Can't get home, can I?" She took a few hesitant steps in his direction.

"No. Better to call your mother and tell her what's going on."

She nodded and pulled out her phone from her bag. "At least there's service now."

To give her privacy, he retreated to the living area and sank onto the plush armchair. He could hear her soft voice as she spoke on the phone.

The sound both comforted and tormented him as he thought about their lovemaking, his proposal, and her rejection.

Too fast? They'd both waited a decade and a half.

He waited for Koreen to finish her call. As soon as she was done, she walked into the living area, clutching her bag and hobbling a little on her heels. "Sorry to have kept you waiting. Mama is on her own, so…"

"It's fine. Is she okay, though? Does she need anything?"

"Our area rarely ever floods, thank goodness. She's alright, just worried about me. She wanted to talk to you and say thanks, but I told her you're in a separate room." She flushed a little as she spoke, her eyes meeting his for a moment before darting away.

In a different world, they would damn well be engaged by now.

"You can tell her whatever you like, Koreen. I don't really mind."

"Um, listen…I can find a cheaper room or something,

so I won't be a bother." She looked uneasy as she spoke, fidgeting a little with her bag.

"No." His response was immediate and just as forceful, surprising even himself. "You can stay here. Use the bedroom. I'll sleep on the couch."

It was the least he could do since she couldn't get home because of the storm. He'd give her the greatest comforts he could offer. He wanted to keep her close, too, selfishly, even if it was just for a little while longer.

"You don't have to do that. Besides, it was my decision to stay last night…" Her voice trailed off, her cheeks reddening a little more.

He didn't answer. Instead, he watched as she looked down at herself, her rumpled black dress from the previous night clinging to her body.

"Do I look okay? This is a bit much for lunch, isn't it?"

He took in her appearance, strong and beautiful, pained to see her so unsure of herself. "No, it's fine. You look perfect." He hesitated before adding, "The world should be yours, Koreen."

She shook her head, dismissing the compliment. But he could tell it had affected her, the color on her face still evident. "Are you ready to go eat?"

She nodded, and he offered her his arm. The elevator ride was silent and charged, like a bomb waiting to rip their world apart.

When they reached the lobby, the hotel manager greeted them with apologies for the storm. Royce waved off his concerns, insisting that the storm was beyond anyone's control.

The manager nodded, turning his attention to Koreen.

"We are very sorry Miss Cisco can't get a car, but we will provide everything she needs during her stay."

"Thank you." Koreen smiled and thanked him, her manners impeccable. Royce felt oddly proud to see her so composed.

As they walked and took their seat at the restaurant, he watched her and the other guests 'stormed in' right along with them. In sharp contrast to the silence between him and Koreen, everyone else in the dining room was talking animatedly.

They both ate without speaking; the clink of silverware on plates their only exchange. She seemed to enjoy the meal, eating heartily despite the heavy atmosphere. He was pleasantly surprised to see her appetite match his.

They matched each other in so many ways, both pronounced and intimate.

"Are you okay?" he asked gently, breaking the silence once he had signed the bill.

She nodded. "Thank you for the meal."

"You're welcome. Do you need anything else? What would you like to do? There's a gym and an indoor pool. There are books in the gift shop, too."

"I'd like to make time to read again soon," she said, a little wistfully.

"Reading is one area I can't keep up with you in."

She gave him a small smile. "I used to read mostly shorter romance books and you had a thing for thrillers, so there's really no comparison, is there? I remember you liked John Grisham a lot. You wanted to be that lawyer in *A Time to Kill*."

The fact that she could recall his favorite book growing up was more than enough to break his heart. "I got a signed copy from the author. One of my friends in Saudi got me one for my thirtieth birthday."

"That's so cool. I'd like to see it someday."

At the back of his mind, he knew that someday might never come.

Another awkward silence settled between them. The other guests in the dining room slowly trickled out, sharing their concerns about the storm and showing each other photos on their phones.

"We can have a look at the books in the shop," he offered.

She shook her head. "It's okay. I should go back to the room and get some sleep. I should call my brother and some of my friends to check on them."

As they made their way towards the elevators, her phone rang. She glanced at the screen before answering.

"Hey, Leo."

In the relative silence of the elevator, Royce could hear Leo Tuazon's voice on the other end.

"Hey, Koreen. Just wanted to check if you're okay. Are you at home?"

"No...I'm stuck somewhere else. With a friend. How about you?"

"I'm at home. It's not so bad here in Molo, but I'm closing the gym for at least a few days. The whole area is flooded, and I'm pretty sure the ceiling would have leaked by now if it hasn't already caved in."

"I'm so sorry, Leo."

"It's okay. You know how it is."

"Have you heard from the others?"

"Jonah went to Maggie's last night before it got too bad in Tagbac. Ace and his family are okay."

She sighed in relief. "We're all safe. That's what matters, right?"

"Yeah. We'll just have to deal with whatever comes our way next."

"Stay safe. Let me know if you need any help."

"You, too. I'll be in touch once the storm clears. Take care."

Koreen exchanged goodbyes with Leo before she hung up. She replaced the phone in her bag and was quiet the rest of the way.

Once they reached the penthouse, she immediately noticed a basket of fresh clothes provided by the hotel. "Oh, wow. I really didn't expect this."

"Please, make yourself comfortable." He tried to keep his voice steady despite the pang of longing that almost caused him physical pain. If it were up to him, she wouldn't need any clothes.

Now they behaved as if they were strangers stuck in a room together. He watched her carry the basket into the bedroom, shutting the door behind her. Minutes later, he could hear the muffled sound of the shower. He wanted nothing more than to join her.

But he'd fucked it all up, hadn't he?

Royce settled behind the desk set up in the living area and opened his laptop. Work was always a reliable means of escape. He sent emails to his assistant and managers, the clack of the keyboard momentarily drowning out his thoughts of the woman only one wall apart but seemingly worlds away from him. As the afternoon went on, he could hear the faint murmur of the television from the bedroom.

As the gray day gave way to a pitch-black night, Royce

finally closed his laptop, having exhausted himself with work. He stood up, stretching his limbs before checking on Koreen.

She had fallen asleep on the bed while watching Netflix. An episode of *Cobra Kai* was still playing at low volume.

He slowly approached the bed and pulled the blankets around her sleeping form. He switched off the TV and closed the blinds, plunging the room into darkness.

"Goodnight, Koreen," he said.

He tried to stop himself then, but even his pride could not hold him back from saying the words he'd wanted to confess for so long.

He might never have the chance to tell her again.

"I love you. I always have, and I always will."

ELEVEN

Koreen

RECOMPENSE

WHERE WAS SHE?

It took Koreen a few seconds to get her bearings as she stirred awake, still wrestling with the leaden weight of her dreams. Her face felt cold with moisture; as she reached up to touch the skin, she realized they were teardrops.

She willed her eyes to focus as she fumbled under the pillows for her phone. Her hands closed around the ice-cold device quickly, only to find out it had gone dead while she slept.

With a sigh, she reached over to her side and managed to switch the lamp on. A quick glance at the hotel phone revealed it was almost one in the morning.

Even with the protection of the comforter, she shivered.

The temperature had dropped significantly since she'd gone to bed, and she was clad only in the plain white underwear provided by the hotel. Her eyes scanned the room, landing on two light dresses that hung on the closet door, which she'd unearthed from the complimentary basket earlier. They looked like something one might wear to the beach, not in a freezing suite in the middle of a typhoon.

She went into the bathroom and tried to put on the robe but found it still damp from her earlier shower. Frustration gnawed at her as she fumbled through the closet, fingers finally brushing against a soft cotton t-shirt. Realizing it belonged to Royce, she hesitated for a moment before pulling it over her head, desperate for warmth.

Memories from the previous night flooded her mind; their bodies entwined, having each other until dawn. The scent of him still lingered on her, from the bed they had previously shared.

He was outside, wasn't he? He'd said earlier that he'd sleep on the couch.

She needed to see him, even if it was just for a moment.

Her steps silent on the plush carpet, she padded across the suite to the living area. She paused in the doorway, her breath catching at the sight before her.

In the dim lamplight, she could see Royce asleep on the couch, clad only in shorts, oblivious to the chill around them. He looked a little awkward crammed onto the cushions, his long legs and large frame a little too big even for the oversized couch.

The blinds of the floor-to-ceiling windows had been left open, revealing the shadows and lights of the darkened, waterlogged city around them. Guilt and regret descended on her as she watched his chest rise and fall with each slow breath. Her fingers itched to touch and trace his muscles.

Royce stirred, as if knowing he was being watched, one hand reaching into the semi-darkness for something—or someone. All she had to do was step closer and she would be in his arms again.

The arms of the vulnerable-looking, half-naked man before her, who had bared his heart to her and offered everything he had, everything he was.

They had always competed against each other and trained together, ever since they were children, but he'd never been cruel to her or treated her badly. He'd always treated her like a gentleman. She was the one who had kept pushing him away, afraid of losing herself to her own feelings.

Fuck it all.

Her hands clenched into fists, wanting to hit something so badly in frustration as she recalled the way he'd looked at her on the football field, trying to tell her something she hadn't been ready to hear. But now...it was too late, even if she listened.

He had already reached a point in their lives where she'd never be his equal. He had the world now, while all she had were memories and the burgeoning realization of her love for him.

A love she would cut clean, too. She had already decided she wouldn't accept the job at Boundless. She had her life, and he had his.

She knelt beside his sleeping form on the couch. Up close, she could see that his beard had grown uneven. She found comfort in its imperfection. It made him seem more human, less untouchable.

"Hey," she whispered, reaching out to touch his cheek. "I'm sorry, I fell asleep."

"Uh," Royce mumbled, shaking off sleep. His eyes widened slightly in surprise, perhaps at her unexpected tenderness. "It's okay."

"Did you have dinner?"

"No, but I'm fine." He rubbed his eyes as he slowly pulled himself up to a seated position.

"Would you like me to call downstairs for some food?" she offered hesitantly.

"It's okay; I'd rather sleep." The smile on his face looked forced. "Work knocked me out."

Koreen nodded, pained at the awkwardness between them. It was as if they were strangers, tiptoeing around each other's feelings. "Maybe you should move to the bed. It's more comfortable. I can sleep here. You could fit two of me on this thing."

Royce shook his head. Her heart ached at the distance that stretched between them, even if they were shoulder-to-shoulder. She wondered if he could see it in her gaze.

To distract herself, she reached for a bottle of water on the coffee table and opened it before gently slipping it into his hand.

"Have some water."

"Thanks."

As he drank, she embraced his arm, urging him to move to the bed. He hesitated, then declined once more.

It was a stubbornness she knew and understood all too well. Neither of them were willing to concede their independence.

But then they both gave way, just a little.

"Stay here with me," he said, putting the empty bottle down on the side table and holding out his arm to her.

It was a beautiful surprise, like a parting gift. She knew this might very well be their last night together.

"Okay." She scooted over and curled up next to him, welcoming the warmth of his body against hers. She listened to the rhythm of his heartbeat, its steadiness grounding her to this fleeting moment.

One last night with him. A memory I could lock away in my heart.

As if sensing her thoughts, he pulled her closer.

"Koreen, I…." His voice was hesitant, but his gaze never left hers. "I've dreamt of this moment—seeing you come to me, wearing my shirt. I bet every man has this kind of fantasy."

He could not have hit her any harder.

The tears she'd been holding back for hours finally welled up in her eyes, spilling down her cheeks. He reached out, wiping them away with his thumb.

"It's okay," he murmured as he pulled her back into his arms.

Finally, Koreen cried.

She cried for the kind boy who had bought her all the fishball she wanted to eat and given her a twenty-peso bill; the young man who had stolen her heart and bound her to him with a black belt and a white anemone.

She cried for the man he had become.

The man who now held her so tenderly; a man who conquered her heart, body and soul in one fell swoop.

She didn't know how long she cried; the shadows danced before her eyes as his whispers and caresses became tender music to her senses, a tune she would never forget.

When she was finally spent, she allowed herself to melt into him, committing to memory the feel of his body pressed against hers.

"I promise, I'm not going to ask you to marry me again." Royce's voice sounded as if she were underwater. "Let's just be here together until our time is up. No strings attached."

"I'd like that." She reached up, this time trying to memorize the angles of his face with her touch.

"Can I tell you what's going to happen when the storm's over?"

She nodded.

"When it's over, you're going to go home. And I'm sure you're going to tell me you're not accepting the job at Boundless."

She didn't have the energy for denial. "How did you know?"

He smiled sadly, brushing a strand of hair from her face. "I know you better than anyone, Koreen. You're a queen—you go all or nothing. You run the world as you'd have it, not the way I'd want it to be."

Her heart swelled with love and admiration for this man who understood her so completely. Wordlessly, she nodded.

"I have to be honest, too. I wanted this so much. I'm sorry if I came on too strong. That was never my intention. I only wanted to show you what I could give."

"Please don't apologize," she said, her words muffled against his shoulder.

"Okay." With that, he pulled her up to his lap, burying his face in her hair.

Nothing more was said.

As morning drew closer, she felt their breathing syncing with each other's as they slowly drifted towards sleep.

Koreen stirred first, tugging at his hand as her feet found the carpet. "Come to bed. You should rest."

"Alright." There was a hint of weariness in his voice but he followed as she led him to the bed, guided by the soft glow of the bathroom light she'd left on earlier.

They stretched out next to each other, eyes locking, before she inched closer to him, seeking his warmth once more.

He pulled the covers over them and hesitated for a moment before asking, "Can I hold you? Like last night?"

She could feel a bittersweet smile form on her lips as she nodded her assent. There was no place else she would rather be. As his warmth seeped into her own skin, she turned her face towards him, her eyes meeting his. "I'm sorry, Royce. I'm really sorry."

He shushed her with a kiss on her nose. "You said no more apologizing, right?"

"Right."

"Then don't be sorry, Koreen." He reached for her hair, combing his fingers through the strands with an almost reverent air. "Just let me love you, like last night, too."

"Please," she whispered.

He kissed her deeply, his tongue dancing with hers as he cradled her face between his hands. She put her arms around his neck, as if clinging to a beautiful dream.

This was the dream that made her cry.

Everything else around them faded away, leaving only their passion, tempered by longing and hurt and the inevitability of time. It was a slow exploration, a rediscovery of one another.

She felt his hands trace her body, his touch gentle yet unyielding, his desire evident in the way he held her as he took her over and over again.

Her own fingers roamed across his skin, reacquainting herself with his sheer power, his steady strength. She held on to him as tightly as she could, giving in to the need and pleasure that he coaxed from her body, allowing herself to drown in his kisses and his touch.

In those moments, she allowed herself to believe that, after a lifetime of competition and then separation, they were meant to be together.

But the dream had to end.

The first light of dawn began to filter through the curtains, signaling the end of the storm. As they lay entwined, spent in their desperation, time seemed to slow, too, as if reluctant to break them apart.

She knew the world outside would, soon enough, rear its cruel head. She knew she would be made to believe, yet again, that nothing lasts forever.

Not nothing.

Koreen Cisco knew how to one-up fate, too.

My love would last forever.

For the final time, she took Royce in her arms, whispering his name, etching every sensation and emotion deep into her heart, where her memories would remain long after the sun had risen.

Long after they had said goodbye.

TWELVE

Royce

REMAINDER

HIS WORLD MOVED AT A RELENTLESS PACE, AND TIME was a ruthless taskmaster.

For Royce, the days and nights ebbed and flowed into one another. He used to be fueled by dogged determination and unabashed ambition; now, he moved out of habit.

He knew if he stopped, it would be the end of him. So he didn't.

He took in the progress that had been made since the typhoon finally left Iloilo City. The construction site of Boundless Tower stretched out before him, the chaos of cranes and trucks filling the air with a cacophony of mechanical

He hadn't allowed himself much time for reflection these past few weeks, as he had been working nonstop—changing schedules, making arrangements, and ensuring that everything would be back on track as soon as possible.

In the wake of the storm, he'd made the best decision he could.

As soon as air travel was possible again, he'd called in two of his best: Jesse Lozada, who managed Boundless Jeddah, and Kotaro Yoshida, his personal assistant.

He'd appointed Lozada, a fellow Filipino from the neighboring region of Cebu, as the manager of Boundless Philippines. Yoshida followed shortly, meant to stay in Iloilo for a few weeks to provide support.

"Royce-san." Yoshida appeared next to him, clad in safety gear. The young Japanese man lowered his head respectfully. "Do you really wish to leave the Philippines so soon?"

He was speaking Nihongo, a subtle sign that the conversation would veer towards more personal territory.

Royce inclined his head and gave a small smile. "Your concern is appreciated, Yoshida, but this is for the best. We have more business to bring in and more operations centers to build."

"Ah, but Prince Khalid made it very clear he wishes for you to stay longer," said Yoshida delicately. "He has given orders for you to take a vacation at the company's expense. Rushing back to work will displease him."

"I'm not rushing back. I will be staying with my parents for a few days in Manila. I need to return to Saudi to appoint Lozada's successor. You know this."

"Nine years away is a very long time," Yoshida went on,

his eyes lowered in deference. "I have served you for six years, and I have never seen you take a break."

"Thank you for your honesty, Kotaro-san, but my decision is final. I'm sure you and Lozada will keep things running smoothly here."

Yoshida nodded and didn't press the matter any further. "Of course, sir. I have also confirmed with your lawyer that the investment offer is in place. As soon as the other party signs the contract, the funds will be wired. In fact, the funds are ready now."

"Good. Please have Attorney Panes contact them after I have left the country."

"Of course, sir." Yoshida reverted smoothly to English, bowing again. "I wish you safe travels. If there are any changes to your schedule, I will ring you immediately."

"Thank you, Yoshida. I'll see you back in Saudi."

After his assistant had said goodbye and disappeared back into the construction site, Royce slowly made his way out, surveying the damage that the place had sustained from the storm. The ground was still muddy and uneven, but overall, the situation seemed manageable.

Lozada was waiting for him by the hire car, standing with an air of confidence and a big smile that immediately put Royce at ease. A BPO veteran who had supervised some of the earliest call centers and transcription facilities in the Middle East, he'd been all too happy to finally work in his home country.

"Leaving us so soon, sir?"

"I've done what I needed to do in Iloilo, Jesse. It's your turn now."

Lozada didn't mince words. "Well, I'm happy to report

that it's not as bad as it looks. If there are no more big storms like the one we had weeks back, we could call in more trucks of sand and gravel to patch up the damage and carry on with the construction. I've been talking to the engineers and they told me the ground is quite stable. I've also scheduled another team to have a look after the weekend; one of them worked on our Pune site, too."

"Very good. And the recruits?"

"Already taken care of," Lozada assured him. "We've finalized our schedule at the Convention Center to begin orientations for the new staff. Hands-on training will take place at a computer college in the city during nighttime after classes. They have equipment our recruits could train on in the meantime."

"Keep me posted daily, Jesse," Royce said, clapping him on the shoulder. "I made the right decision bringing you home."

"Thank you, sir." Lozada's face broke into a wide grin. "I'm just glad to be back in the Philippines. My wife and children are excited to come to Iloilo."

"I'm happy for you and your family." Royce held out his hand; the other man took it and shook firmly. "Thank you again for everything."

"You're welcome, boss." Lozada stepped aside as the driver opened the car door for Royce.

"Take care of Boundless here for me, Jesse," Royce said through the window, giving the other man a nod in farewell.

"I will. I won't let you down." Lozada gave a jaunty wave. "Safe travels!"

As the car pulled away from the busy construction site, Royce watched the sunset illuminate the unfinished skeleton of Boundless Tower. In his mind's eye, he could already see the strong yet elegant and graceful lines of the completed skyscraper. It had been designed to mimic the appearance of a queen, proud and regal.

Koreen would have been perfect here.

He had imagined her managing this facility, with her impeccable background in the industry, her incomparable work ethic, and, most of all, her fierce dedication to excellence.

In another life, she would have been his wife, his queen. But she had always followed her own path, and he couldn't help but respect her for that.

The sky was already a deep, velvety blue when Royce arrived at the hotel. He knew work was still ongoing at the Tower, with its construction in multiple shifts. He would have wanted to stay longer, but he took comfort in the presence of Lozada and Yoshida there. They were men he could trust with the project.

It was time for him to leave; the rest of the world awaited him. He would be alone, once again, but then that was the world he'd built, wasn't it? It kept moving, waiting for no one.

As he made his way across the lobby, his gaze fell upon a familiar face seated on one of the plush beige sofas near reception.

Kenneth Cisco stood up with a broad smile and made his way over. The years had not dulled his quickness. Before Royce could adequately react, the other man had pulled him in for a tight bear hug.

"Duran! So good to see you, man!"

Royce recovered by giving him a thump on the back. "Good to see you, too, Doc."

They had been friends and basketball buddies since

elementary school. Kenneth was two years younger but a great player, a wily point guard who'd commanded Royce's respect.

Kenneth stepped back and regarded him curiously. "You look like one of those rich princes from Dubai. Which car do you drive again?"

"A *Mercedes S*," he answered automatically. It took him a second to realize that the younger man was joking. "Fuck, you were kidding, weren't you?"

Kenneth chuckled. "You are serious. Damn. I was pretty sure you had one of those. I wasn't wrong, was I?"

"You hit it right on the head," Royce conceded. "What brings you here, Doc? I'm glad I got to see you before I leave tomorrow. My flight's at eight in the morning."

"Tomorrow? Already? We didn't even get the chance to have that game with the gang. Damn typhoon had me stuck in San Jose. Couldn't travel with all the flooding and landslides on the road."

"There's already someone running the Philippine operations of our company, so it's time for me to go." It wasn't completely true, but it would have to do. "No rest for the wicked and all that."

"Yeah, sounds about right." Kenneth smiled, glancing at his watch. "I have to pick up my girlfriend at eight. Do you think you can spare an old friend an hour for a drink? I promise not to drink you under the table like I did last time when we won that summer league championship. The fun of underage drinking."

"One drink," Royce relented with a laugh. "I barely drink these days."

"One drink, then," Kenneth agreed.

They went to the hotel bar, settling into chairs by the

window overlooking the city. Royce made Kenneth pick the drink. They ordered Black Label whiskey.

"I'm glad I made it on time before you left," Kenneth said as soon as their glasses had arrived. "I'm only in town for the weekend to see my girlfriend and family, so I thought I'd drop by to say hello. I have to be back at the hospital early Monday morning."

"Let's drink to the time we have now, then." Royce raised his glass.

"Cheers." Kenneth lifted his own glass and met his with a resounding clink.

They sipped their whiskey in companionable silence for a few minutes, watching bolts of lightning skitter across the early evening sky.

"I believe thanks are in order, too," said Kenneth casually. "I have to thank you for looking after my sister during the storm."

Royce swallowed his sip of whiskey; a little too hard it scalded its way into his throat. He hoped Kenneth hadn't noticed his wince of pain.

"Don't mention it," he replied in what he hoped was a dismissive tone. "We had dinner to catch up. Before anyone knew it, no one could get a car in or out of the hotel."

"Still." Kenneth tipped his glass in his direction. "Our mother was worried sick, but she was very reassured that Koreen was stuck here with you.

Royce shrugged, forcing a smile. He wasn't quite sure how Kenneth—or his mother—would react if he knew the truth. "I'm glad I could help."

"By the way, Royce, how did you survive two nights with Koreen?"

The question was meant to tease, but memories of those nights—his body entwined with Koreen's, his lips on hers, his hands on her skin, himself inside her—threatened Royce's composure. "Koreen was fine, no trouble at all. She spent most of her time eating and watching *Cobra Kai*."

"I'm surprised you got her to slow down," said Kenneth, chuckling lightly. "She's always on the move—teaching here, working there. Did she try to use your computer to run an online class or something?"

Royce shook his head. "Never once mentioned it."

"Wow." Kenneth shook his head incredulously. "Perhaps the storm happened for a reason, just to hold her down for a while."

"How is she now? Still keeping busy, I bet." The question had to be asked, or Kenneth might start wondering what had really happened during those stormed-in nights.

Kenneth sighed. "Yeah, she jumped right back onto the swing of things once she could drive around town again. She was actually the one who dropped me off here."

"I see. She's got one of those transcription classes, then?" He was quite sure Koreen had not mentioned to her own brother—or anyone else—about the job offer at Boundless and her subsequent refusal to accept it.

"She was going to the gym. I think she's training some kids for a tournament. They're all working late these days, to make up for when the gym was closed for a week."

"Yeah. I heard her talking to Leo about the gym taking damage during the storm."

As they went back to sipping their drinks, Royce's thoughts went back to the morning the storm ended.

He had held Koreen in his arms as they watched the sun

rise over the flooded city. They had breakfast at the restaurant, subdued and peppered only with small talk. An imposing four-wheel drive with an equally no-nonsense driver had then appeared on the driveway, sent by the owner of the hotel for Royce to use as he pleased.

Their separation had been simple and bittersweet. The last thing he could recall doing was kissing her on the forehead before helping her into the massive black vehicle. She had touched his cheek lightly before she'd pressed her lips against his skin. The last thing he remembered seeing was her in a pink sundress, a scarf awkwardly draped around her shoulders, waving goodbye to him with a tiny smile on her lips.

"You were always good for Koreen, Royce," Kenneth said earnestly, interrupting his thoughts. "I mean, I couldn't say anything all those years ago; I was a kid, but now…"

"What do you mean, Doc?"

Kenneth shrugged. "You've always kind of looked after her when we were growing up. You're pretty much the big brother we both needed, really. "

Royce shifted in his seat, feeling the weight of the words. "What makes you say that? Koreen and I have been competing all our lives."

"Competing?" Kenneth scoffed, shaking his head. "Man, you were looking out for her. You were always in the same space where she was, just to make sure she wasn't alone. That's a real man."

Kenneth's voice was tinged with nostalgia and admiration as he spoke, never taking his eyes off Royce. "Our father, God rest his soul, always praised you for being there for Koreen. Remember that time I got dengue and was hospitalized for more than a month? Fuck, I almost died back then."

Unable to speak past the tightness in his throat, Royce nodded.

"Koreen told us you were there for her, especially when she competed in the junior kata championships for the first time. You're the reason she made it through. You were looking after her the whole time. That's something."

Royce stared into his glass, the amber liquid swirling and dancing in the dim light of the bar. For a few moments, he lost himself in the memory of being eleven years old: walking Koreen to the jeepney stop after practice, asking his mother to make an extra sandwich for her, giving her as much of his meager allowance as he could.

It was love—that very act of caring for her, protecting her, and making sure she was safe. At eleven years old, he knew he loved that fiery girl who had always challenged him. And he…he'd just always wanted to be with her.

"That's a long time ago," Royce said, setting his glass down on the table. The sound seemed to echo through the hushed conversations around them. "We were kids."

Kenneth nodded. "Yeah, we were kids. But sometimes I'd like to think that some things never change. Makes us who we are, right?"

As they sipped their drinks and night descended over the city, they let memories wash over them: their old group, the friends they'd made, and all the tournaments they'd played. Life was much simpler back then, when all they had to worry about were grades, girls, and basketball games.

Kenneth checked his watch and sighed as he set down his empty glass on the table. "I have to get going. I'm picking up my girlfriend from the hospital. She's got a residency here in Iloilo, lucky for her."

"Of course." Royce gestured to a nearby waiter for their bill. "This one's on me."

"Alright, man, but next time I'm taking you to the coast for some good old beer and videoke." Kenneth leaned back in his chair and gave him a mischievous look. "Since you're treating, I'm going to tell you a secret about Koreen."

"A secret? I'm not sure I'm the right person to share these things with." Royce tapped his credit card on the machine offered by the waiter.

Kenneth laughed. "Oh, but you're the perfect person."

As soon as the waiter was out of earshot, Kenneth carried on gleefully. "Don't worry, it's nothing incriminating. Just a little insight into how she thinks."

Curiosity got the better of him. "What's the secret?"

"Did you know that Koreen deliberately failed her Calculus final in your last year of high school? She didn't flunk, of course—her grades were too high for that—but she brought down her grade low enough so you could catch up. You both ended up having the same average, both becoming valedictorians."

Stupefied at the revelation, Royce could only stare. "When—and how—did you find out?"

Kenneth grinned. "Just before they announced the honor roll for your graduation. I overheard her talking to her best friend Dara in her room. The principal had talked to her about it or something, maybe asked her what happened. Koreen was crying, but she kept telling Dara it was worth it. 'He' was worth it." He used his hands to form quotation marks, emphasizing the pronoun.

Shock descended on Royce. "Why would she do that?"

"I told you, you're good for her. She slows down, brings

herself back down to earth. She doesn't want to be alone at the top, man. It's lonely up there."

"But…this doesn't even make any sense. She would never fail a Math test."

"You know how Koreen is. She can do whatever she sets her mind to. On top of that, she only does what she wants. Who knows what goes on in that big brain of hers." Kenneth shrugged, rubbing the back of his neck. "But for you, she did a total one-eighty without even thinking. She made you valedictorian, too, I think, so she wouldn't be alone. I don't think she'd do it for anyone else."

The weight of Kenneth's words settled heavily on Royce's shoulders, and for a moment, he was speechless.

How had he never realized just how deeply their bond ran?

Finally, he found his voice. "I think I should say goodbye to her before I leave. Sounds like the right thing to do, doesn't it?"

"Definitely." Kenneth stood up and held out his hand. "She should be at the gym until eight or something, if I heard her correctly."

He stood up, too, and shook Kenneth's hand. "Thanks, man."

"Keep in touch, okay? And don't stay away too long."

Royce nodded. "I'll do my best. If you or your family need anything, I'm just a message away."

With a strong slap on his back and an energetic goodbye, Kenneth was gone, disappearing into the Friday night crowd of the hotel bar.

Alone to confront his thoughts in the wake of his

discovery, he decided there was no more time for him and Koreen to keep on pretending, hiding, or denying.

She had to know how he really felt. He owed it to her, to himself, and their shared history. He was going to break down every single wall between them, until there was nothing left but the truth.

Because he knew, at the very heart of it all, there was love.

It was a love everyone saw except for them. A love that had bloomed in childhood and grown alongside them; a rivalry that wasn't truly a rivalry at all. It was two people constantly seeking each other, bound by an invisible thread that stretched across the walls and distances that kept them physically apart. Where one was, the other had to be, too.

Koreen had already given in to its power many years ago—and he never knew until tonight.

With hurried strides, he made his way to reception and asked for his car. As he waited, rain began to fall, soft droplets that left a damp chill in the air.

When his car arrived, Royce slid into the backseat and gave the driver directions to the gym. As they drove off into the night, the drizzle intensified.

At the back of his mind, he registered the potential impact of the inclement weather on Boundless Tower's construction, but this fleeting thought was quickly swallowed by the urgency of seeing her again.

Koreen.

The rain was already falling in torrents, punctuated by cracks of lightning and loud thunderclaps, by the time they reached the gym's street. As the Tuazon school came into view, Royce spotted a lone red Corolla parked in front. He remembered her car from his session at the gym weeks ago;

he'd seen her get into it with about half a dozen duffel bags and drive off.

Relieved and overwhelmed, he dismissed the driver for the night once his feet hit the pavement. His pulse quickened as he, oblivious that he was drenched head to toe, ran up the steps. He had no idea there were so many.

He tried to catch his breath as he stepped onto the worn blue carpet of the reception area. There were barely any lights on. He couldn't see or hear anyone in the facility.

The place was empty, except for Koreen.

Illuminated by the white fluorescent bulbs, she stood alone in the enclosed training area where they had done the kata together weeks ago. Her back was turned to the entryway as she erased notes from the whiteboard. She was still clad in her karategi.

"Hey, Asha, forgot something?" she called out, vigorously rubbing out lines written in black marker. "You left your Squishmallow. I kept Shantira with me. I know how much you love her."

She turned, eraser still in hand, smiling and pointing to a fluffy blue toy draped over her bag on the floor. "She's right there—"

Her voice caught when she saw him, shock and confusion flickering across her face.

"Hi, Koreen."

"Royce? What the hell are you doing here?" Her cheeks flushed a deep shade of pink, her eyes wide with surprise.

"I...I just want to ask you something."

He saw her take in his drenched appearance; he was still half-breathless from his mad dash through the rain and up the steps. He probably looked like a crazed stalker. If she beat him up right then and there, he couldn't blame her.

"What is it?" Her voice was shaking.

Was she afraid?

He braced himself for the worst—her fists, the eraser, even the whiteboard—but he kept on speaking.

"Does she know how much I love her?"

THIRTEEN

Koreen

RETRACE

This was the dream that made her cry.

She remembered it now.

She'd first dreamed it at the hotel, in the big bed that had witnessed their seemingly insatiable passion.

She'd dreamt it again in the weeks that followed. After ten or more restless nights in a row, she'd taken the black cardboard cut-out and the dried anemone out of the picture frame and kept them in her bag, with every intention of throwing both away when she had the chance.

It was a dream of holding Royce Duran in her arms—until he vanished into thin air. In that dream, he was never really there to begin with. She'd imagined it all: his voice, his cool citrus scent, his touch, their lovemaking.

Even in her waking hours, the dream followed her incessantly.

Tonight, he stood before her, chest heaving, raindrops glistening on his skin and hair like tiny diamonds. Of course this was yet another version of that dream.

The real Royce would never be here, at this time, looking like that.

"Koreen." He spoke again, almost pleadingly, his eyes wild as they seemed to devour the sight of her. "Do you know how much I love you?"

She took a step back, the eraser falling from her grasp as her hands and knees began to shake uncontrollably. "I don't know."

"Do you want to know?"

She held up her hands. If only he'd have mercy and stay away. "Let's not do this."

"Not do this? My flight's tomorrow. I can't leave Iloilo again without telling you the truth. Do you want us to do this in another fifteen years?"

She shook her head, pain shooting through her as if he'd just struck her in the solar plexus. "Please, Royce, I don't have the strength to do this all over again."

"Then let me give you mine," he insisted, taking a step towards her. "Why won't you let me in? Why can't we be together?"

"You know why. You're on top of the world now, but I can't go that high. I would lose myself."

"Never." The word was uttered with such raw determination, making her flinch. "You'll be with me."

"I've been the only person I could count on for the past

fifteen years. If I lose that person...what would happen to me?"

He advanced further, reaching out to her with both hands. "Nothing. That's not going to happen. But why can't you be with me? You belong in my world. We belong with each other."

"Your world is perfect," she countered, tears prickling at the corners of her eyes. "It's a glittering dream of wealth and power...but mine is full of struggle and uncertainty. All my dreams keep slipping away. You were the first to slip away—and I couldn't stop you. Since we were kids, I tried to keep you with me, wherever I was. You made me feel whole, as if you're the best parts of myself. When I was with you, I was always better, happier, stronger. When I lost you, I didn't know what to do."

She felt a tear escape, tracing a hot path down her cheek before she could stop it. She put her arms around her body, fearing she'd fall apart into pieces too small to put back together.

"You know what happens when you take out someone's heart, right? They stop breathing. That's what happened when you left. With Papa gone, too, I quit Karate...I only came back because they gave me a job. In college, I never even made it to the dean's list. It didn't matter that much, because you weren't around. I just ended up working, day after day...until I couldn't stop."

"Koreen...why the fuck didn't you tell me? You should have just called and told me to come back to you."

She shook her head. "A little too late for that, isn't it? Look at what you've achieved. Everything you are now...I don't have a place in a world like yours."

His eyes flashed angrily, his jaw clenching so hard his face looked distorted. "But you do. All of this won't mean anything if you're not with me. I pushed myself to be the man you deserved to have."

"Why would you do that?"

His impatience mounted; she drew back as she saw fury ignite in his eyes. Without warning, Royce stalked towards her, grabbing her arms firmly before she could react. Tears streamed down her face, but he was relentless.

"Because I love you. I loved you before I even understood what it meant. I loved you since we were children, since Shihan Tuazon paired us up and told me you were the best in kata, and I could only hope to be half as good as you."

Royce's grip softened as he continued, his voice so quiet it was barely a rumble in her ear. "He made us training partners because he knew you would challenge me, that you'd make me better. And he was right—you did. All those years, we made each other better. Now, give me a reason why we shouldn't be with each other for the rest of our lives."

Through her tears, she looked into his blazing eyes and shrank back from the intensity she saw, only to be held in place by his unyielding arms.

This was the person she had loved her entire life.

She took in his scent, the mingling of his sweat and the pouring rain around them, and listened to the racing of his heart. She knew in that moment that the heart in that powerful body of his had always been hers.

That heart didn't know the meaning of giving up.

"I...I don't want to lose you again," she whispered, leaning into his embrace, allowing herself to collapse against his chest.

It was everything she had ever wanted. To be loved by the only person she had ever wanted to love her.

"You won't." His answer was immediate, firm, giving no quarter for doubt. "You never fucking will."

"I should have told you that I loved you, all those years ago," she said, a little wistfully. "I didn't know how to. I was too afraid…I didn't want to be weak. I didn't want you to laugh at me."

He cradled her face in his hands, his thumbs brushing away the tear tracks on her cheeks. To her surprise, there were drops of moisture trickling down his face, too. Sweat, tears, or rain—she wasn't sure, but she didn't really care.

"Do you still love me, Koreen?"

She smiled, unable to help herself. "Yes. I love you more now."

"Damn it to hell, woman." He uttered a few more curse words as he sank to his knees before her, wrapping his arms around her waist, burying his face in her stomach. "Was that so fucking hard to say?"

She giggled, euphoria coursing through her as she embraced him right back, her nose burrowing into his short-cropped hair. It tickled, causing another stream of teary giggles.

"No. I know exactly what I want from you, too."

His eyes widened as he lifted his head and looked into her eyes. "And what's that?"

She looked down at him; this strong, intelligent man who never gave up on her; the boy who had looked after her when she was alone; the boy who had been too afraid to say his feelings, too. And now, the man he had become—brave enough to tell her the truth.

"All I've ever wanted was you, Royce." The echo of his words from the hotel proposal resonated within her, reminding her of how desperately they had both longed for each other. Their bodies had been more straightforward, knowing exactly what the other wanted. "I don't need anything else. You've always been enough for me, from the beginning. More than enough."

"You got me. I've been yours since we were six years old, you know."

She took his face in her hands, her fingers tracing the shape of his beard. "Maybe all we ever needed was each other, from the very start."

"You're right," he said softly. "That's all we've ever needed."

"Can I...can I have you, then? Just you?" It was the simplest of questions, causing the most complex mix of emotions inside her: joy, longing, regret, fear. She realized she was trembling, but she knew he was there to hold her up.

He reached up, caressing her cheek tenderly. "You can, Koreen. You never had to ask."

She bent down to kiss him, their lips meeting passionately. The kiss quickly grew heated, their hands hungrily reaching for each other, desperate and feverish after their recent painful separation.

As they kissed, his hands deftly opened her kimono, revealing her camisole and sports bra underneath. He wasted no time in sliding his fingers beneath the layers of fabric, releasing her breasts to the cool night air.

"I miss you," he murmured against her lips, his breath hot and heavy.

"I miss you too," she groaned, feeling heat pool in the pit

of her stomach as she pressed her body tighter against his, her nails digging into his back.

His mouth left hers, trailing a path of hot, open-mouthed kisses down her neck and across her collarbone, finally reaching her breasts. His tongue flicked over her nipples, teasing them as he alternated between licking and sucking.

His hands moved lower, expertly undoing the ties of her pants, allowing them to pool at her feet. He lifted her out of them, leaving her clad only in her underwear and half-open kimono. His eyes roamed over her body as he lowered her damp panties, leaving her completely exposed before him.

He leaned in towards her folds, his breath teasing her sensitive skin. With one hand supporting her waist, he raised her leg slightly, granting his mouth better access. He buried his face between her thighs, his tongue eagerly seeking out her wetness.

The sensation of his lips on her was electrifying; the pleasure he was giving her mounting quickly as she ground against him. She could dimly feel her exposed breasts bouncing as she moved wantonly, but, at the moment, the world was theirs—and theirs alone.

"Please, Royce," she gasped, as she felt the first waves of her climax drawing closer.

Her plea made him redouble his efforts to push her over the edge. His mouth worked in sync with her increasingly desperate movements, bringing her higher and higher, until she couldn't hold back any longer.

"Come for me, my queen," he whispered against her, his tongue flicking over her nub.

That was all she needed. With a final cry of his name, she climaxed, her body trembling with the force of her release.

She collapsed in his arms, momentarily breathless and weak-kneed. He held her easily, his hands rubbing her back, his lips whispering soothing words into her hair.

But that was only the beginning.

As she slowly came to her senses, she felt his hands gently pulling off the rest of her clothes until she stood naked before him. At the corner of her eye, she could see her bare body, proud and glistening, reflected in the mirrors.

She watched as he stood up and swiftly removed his pants, freeing his erection from the confines of his clothing. The sight of him, strong and virile, made her heart race.

"Come here," he commanded as he lowered himself onto the floor once more, opening his legs for her.

She straddled him, feeling the blazing heat of his rock-hard length pressing against her entrance. She put her arms around his neck, using his strength for support as she slowly lowered herself onto him, gasping at the feeling of completeness as he filled her.

She looked into his eyes and saw only burning need. This man…he would have all of her and more.

"Royce, I…" she began, but he silenced her with a kiss.

"Ride me," he urged, his hands gripping her hips as she began to move.

She moaned as she felt him thrust deeper into her, their bodies finding an instinctive rhythm together. This was their own sequence of passion—perfect and powerful.

He licked, caressed, and bit at her breasts as she rose and fell against him, their skin rubbing together deliciously.

"I love you," he breathed between fervent kisses to her neck and chest, his fingers digging into her hips as he drove himself deeper inside her. Her body tightened around him, the intensity of their connection leaving her teetering on the edge of ecstasy.

"I love you, too," she gasped, her orgasm washing over her like a tidal wave. Her head rolled back as the sensations sent her reeling, losing what little control she had left.

Moments later, he followed her over the edge, his body tensing as he poured himself into her, grunting her name into her breasts.

She clung to him as he crashed to the mats, their bodies still entwined. She listened to his heart pounding against her ear, his breath coming in gasps.

"There goes your fifth dan, Sensei," he chuckled breathlessly. "So much for having two champions together, huh?"

"Oh, shut up, you." She gave his shoulder a playful shove, but he caught her hand instead and kissed her palm.

"I love you, Koreen."

"I know." She lowered her head and pressed her lips to his, tasting herself on his mouth.

"You do, don't you?" The desire she could see in his eyes was unmistakable. They weren't done yet; this reunion was too intense, too long-awaited to be satisfied so easily.

He helped her roll off him and pulled her to her feet, a sly grin on his face. "Ready for another round?"

She nodded, not knowing what he had in mind but more than willing to oblige.

Without another word, he swept her into his arms and brought her towards the mirrors that lined one wall of the training area. As soon as he set her down, she ripped off his shirt and jumped onto him, arms around his neck, legs around his hips.

He laughed as he caught her by the waist and peeled her off him. "Later for that, love. I've always wanted to do this."

He set her down so she faced the mirror, and stepped around to stand behind her. She could already feel his hardness against her leg.

"Royce…"

"Hands on the mirror." He gave her a gentle push towards her own reflection, her breasts pressing up against the glass. "Higher."

As she followed his instructions, he drew closer, his chest pressing against her back. His hands roamed down to her heat once more, teasing and coaxing. Her body responded in kind, making him whisper his appreciation against the back of her neck.

His hands found her breasts, his thumbs flicking over the nipples. Her hips bucked, her backside seeking his hardness. She knew now what they were up to.

He entered her from behind, surging into her in one sure, firm stroke. She cried out against the mirror, her body adjusting to his size, the angle new and the mounting pleasure earth-shattering.

He thrust into her and she met him, again and again, their reflections seemingly dancing in the fogged glass as the lights flickered and wavered overhead. The sound of their moans and skin slapping against each other filled the gym, drowned out by rainfall.

"Eyes up, Koreen," he murmured, his voice rough with exertion. "Stay with me. Be with me."

The rest of the world fell away as they locked gazes in the mirror. He didn't miss a beat; he kept up his pace, owning and mastering their rhythm and her. She followed his lead, finally surrendering herself to him.

"Yes, my queen, that's it." His hand slid up front, rubbing her core in firm circles, the pressure of his touch and the friction of his strokes sending her hurtling towards the inevitable.

"Royce...oh god!" She reached the peak in a hoarse scream, her body trembling against the glass.

With a final groan and his deepest thrust, he joined her, his own release exploding within her as he buried his face in her neck, his breath ragged against her skin.

And, outside, the rain grew into a storm.

FOURTEEN

Royce

RESTITUTION

HE WAS HERS NOW.

He felt himself shatter as he thrust deeply into her body. Dimly, he heard his own voice, groaning her name, as his hips gyrated against her backside, unable to let the waves of pleasure subside just yet.

They collapsed together on the floor, their bodies slick with sweat, his arms still around her. She turned to face him, her hands running through his hair, her lips raining kisses on his burning cheeks.

"I love you, Royce," she breathed into his shoulder, still clinging to him like a lifeline.

Their lips met once more, tender and adoring, yet still filled with an insatiable hunger for one another.

"I've always loved you, Koreen," he answered, kissing his way down, from her lips to her jawline, from her chin to her collarbone. He'd missed her sweet strawberry scent so badly.

As reality settled over them, she disentangled her limbs from his and, shyly, gathered her discarded uniform and underwear from the floor. Her cheeks flushed a rosy pink, she giggled as she darted naked towards the locker room, leaving him to pull up his pants and attempt to reassemble his torn shirt.

He gathered her black bag and the blue stuffed toy off the mats and made his way to the main hall of the gym, waiting for her to finish.

A few minutes later, she exited the staff room, dressed in a t-shirt and jeans, her long hair tied back. Illuminated by flickering bulbs and flashes of lightning, she was breathtaking, even more than the night he'd first brought her to the hotel for dinner. He took her into his arms and kissed her.

This time, there was no hesitation on her part as she responded in kind, meeting his lips with her own, just as enthusiastically.

"I've got her," he said, holding up the stuffed animal that had sparked their entire encounter. It was only then that he came to notice it wasn't only a toy; it also had the straps of a backpack.

"Shantira." She smiled affectionately. "She belongs to one of my kata juniors. Asha considers her a lucky charm."

"Asha is right about that. Does she know where I can get my own Shantira—or perhaps a hundred of her, to be sure?"

"I'll ask," she replied with a light laugh, taking the backpack-slash-toy and draping one of its straps over her shoulder. "But, tonight, she's coming with me. With the way the rain's going, I won't be surprised if this part of town floods again soon."

He nodded. "Where do you want to go? Home?"

She looked up into his eyes, reaching over to stroke her thumb over his lips. "I don't really know. I just want to be with you. I...I missed you."

"I missed you, too." He pulled her close. His heart clenched at the thought of him being away from her again, but he didn't want to think about it now. "I'm leaving at eight tomorrow...Tell me what you want to do until then."

She took his hand as she looked at the stormy world through the gym's windows, the rain drumming a relentless rhythm on the roof above them.

"We need to go. If it starts to flood, my car won't be able to get out of this part of the city." She hesitated for a moment. "Maybe I can drive you to the hotel? We can stay there safely from the storm, like before. I don't think I'll be able to get home at this rate."

He felt a smile tug at his lips, at the poignant memories of the precious, fleeting time they had spent together in his room. "Let's do that."

Hand in hand, they descended the steps. Still familiar with the workings of the facility, he pulled down the steel doors over the entryway and waited for her to lock up.

"I hope another storm won't destroy this place." Koreen's voice was tinged with wistful affection as she replaced the keys in her bag and ran her hands over the metal door. "It means so much to so many people."

Royce surveyed the foundations of the building. The ceilings and walls might eventually give in, but the structure itself was inherently tough and stable, made of thick steel and pure gravel from an older time. "Sometimes you have to take damage to see how strong you really are."

With their fingers entwined, they braved the storm together, walking towards her car. The downpour had become much heavier since his arrival at the gym.

She drove through the rain-slicked streets with a determined cast to her face. The windshield wipers fought a losing battle against the pouring rain, but, in the end, they made it through.

Upon arriving at the hotel, they silently agreed to head straight to his room. The moment the door clicked shut behind them, he pulled her into his arms once more.

"Koreen," he whispered. "I have always loved you."

She didn't answer, but her arms went around his stomach as she pressed her face to his chest. He hoped she could hear that his heart knew and spoke only her name.

They stood together in their momentary shelter from the storm, until he gently broke the silence.

"Let's do this properly, my queen. I want to do this right."

He picked up the phone and ordered a big dinner for the both of them. As they waited, they settled in front of the glass windows, watching the cityscape being battered by rain and wind.

The food and drinks arrived, and they ate in comfortable silence, occasionally sharing a smile or a touch.

The unspoken truth of his impending departure hung heavily between them. Somehow, acknowledging it would make it all too real—so neither of them did.

Once they finished eating, Koreen took her phone out and called her mother. He discreetly got out of her way, tidying their plates back onto the trays and placing them outside the main door to be picked up.

When he was done, Royce found her by the wall, plugging in the charger for her phone.

"Is your mother okay?"

She nodded. "Kenneth and Debbie are with her. It's a good thing they decided to bring some dinner home to her."

He took a seat on the couch and opened his arms for her. She joined him and, together, they returned to watching the storm, holding on to each other.

After a while, he spoke, unable to contain his curiosity any longer. "Koreen…is it true that you deliberately flunked our last Calculus exam in high school?

She froze, but she didn't say anything, just turned her face away from his slightly.

"I always did wonder, you know. Your grades were definitely higher than mine during senior year. Something must have happened that made us get the same average in the end. Is it true?"

In the soft light of the living area, he could see a tinge of red on her cheeks. She remained stubbornly silent.

He tried again, sensing the truth behind her evasion. "Did you make yourself fail, so I could catch up?"

"How did you find out?" she demanded, giving him a wary look as she drew back. "Dara was the only one who knew, and she's in the US now."

He reached up and tweaked her nose. "Does it matter?"

She hesitated, pushing his hand away irritably. She crossed her arms over her chest, not meeting his eyes. "Oh, for fuck's sake. Yes, I did."

He tried to pull her back towards him, causing her to

retreat to the other end of the couch. Undeterred, he scooted over and promptly covered her with his body. She tried to push him off, but he used his weight to keep her pinned down.

"Was it worth it?" he murmured, his mouth a few inches away from hers.

"It was," she replied, still avoiding his gaze.

"Koreen."

"What?"

"Love you."

"God, stop it already. You were worth it, okay? I couldn't bear it if you weren't with me. I switched half the integers and misplaced a lot of decimal points. That damn test still haunts me until now. But then, I think of you…and it's okay."

It was his turn to freeze. Kenneth's revelation had surprised him, but the raw, almost angry, honesty in Koreen's admission hit differently.

The depth of her feelings, captured in that simple confession, humbled him.

"Did you know that Dr. Briones actually talked to me about it? I told her I was exhausted and got confused with some of the questions. I don't think she believed me at all, but no one could do anything."

A failure. A white lie. A strike against her own brilliant intellect and reputation.

All for him.

She made another attempt to push him off. He was well aware that she was perfectly capable of breaking his neck or gouging his eyes out from her position, but she didn't. She probably really did love him.

"Royce, I can't breathe. You weigh a ton."

Still dumbstruck, he lifted his body off hers. She slid out

from under him and crossed the room to an armchair, where her black bag sat with Shantira. He watched her pull out a small object and walk back to him.

Instead of sitting down, she stood before him, holding out her hand. In her palm was a battered piece of dark-colored cardboard. "Here."

He finally found his voice, amidst all the shock. "What is it?"

"It's the flower you gave me all those years ago." She unfolded it to reveal a clump of shriveled petals. "Your anemone. You gave it to me in this cardboard box."

"Koreen, I..." The words disappeared in his throat, swallowed by emotions too many to name.

"I used to keep it with your belt," she explained, almost dreamily, as if lost in memory. "Then I kept it with our picture. When I got home from the hotel last time, I took it out."

Her fingers smoothed the dried anemone tenderly. "I've been carrying it with me for weeks. I thought about throwing it away when the time felt right, but that moment never came. I just couldn't let it go. But now I could."

He reached out to touch the fragile petals. So many years, so much time, kept in a single memento.

"Why?" he choked out.

"Because I have you now."

He took the cardboard and the old flower nestled within it from her hand, setting the past aside, carefully, on the coffee table. When he pulled her into his arms, she didn't resist.

"We have each other now," he corrected gently.

She nodded as she nestled against him, all her earlier irritation gone. "I've only ever wanted you, Royce. Not what you have, not what you can give—just you."

He leaned down and captured her lips in a kiss. It started slow and gentle, their mouths barely touching. But the intensity grew quickly, like a wildfire.

They undressed one another, carefully peeling off layer after layer until they were bare in each other's hands. He scooped her up into his arms and carried her to the bed.

She made him lie down next to her, and lost no time by placing tender kisses on his chest before descending further down his body. She knelt between his legs, her fingers lightly stroking him before she slid his length between her lips.

The sensation of her mouth engulfing him sent shockwaves through his entire body. He fought to keep his eyes open, needing to see her as she brought him closer and closer to the edge. The warmth of her breath, the wetness of her tongue, and the rhythmic suction drove him to the brink—and beyond.

"Koreen," he gasped, gripping the heavy wooden headboard so hard he, dimly, heard it crack. He heard nothing more as the intensity of his climax overtook him.

As the last shudders of his orgasm ebbed away, he reached for her, worshipping her skin with caresses and kisses until she was soaking wet and ready.

"We have all night, my queen," he said, burying his face between her breasts. "Let's make the most of it."

She ran her hands down his back as she pushed her hips and chest upward, all his for the taking. "I want that, too."

And so they began, their bodies moving together, exploring every inch of heated skin. Over and over again, they lost themselves in each other.

They made love on the bed, the soft sheets tangling around them as they writhed in rhythm with the rain. They made love on the floor, the plush carpet cushioning their movements as they explored new positions and angles. They made love against the glass windows, the cool surface contrasting with their burning passion, and on the desk, her body draped over the wood as his tongue teased her before he took her again, sinking deeply into her core.

He lost count how many times he had her—it could be ten, or twenty. After a quick shower where he ate her out against the tiles, under a stream of warm water, he carried her back to the bed.

He wasn't sure who dozed off first, but they were awakened by a persistent ringing sound. He thought at first it was his alarm, set for four in the morning.

"Your phone," Koreen muttered as she stirred in his arms, still clinging to him, one leg draped over his hips.

He fumbled sleepily with one hand, reluctant to let her go with the other, before finally locating his mobile on the bedside table.

The name on the display wrenched all the sleep out of him. Royce sat up, bringing Koreen along. She groaned in protest but adjusted her position, still half-asleep.

The clock read a few minutes past three in the morning. He swiped to take the call. "Yoshida."

"I am very sorry to bother you, Mr. Duran." His assistant's voice sounded wide awake.

"It's alright, Yoshida. Everything okay?"

"I have just been informed by the airline that your flight to Manila has been cancelled because of the storm. I tried to find you another, but all flights in and out have been grounded until further notice."

A sense of relief washed over him, followed by a looming

uncertainty in what could come next—the state of Boundless Tower, his decisions in running the company all over the world, his love for and future with the woman in his arms.

"It can't be helped. In the morning, please tell Jesse not to push any work on the Tower until the flood has subsided." Both Yoshida and Lozada were staying in another hotel, closer to the building site.

"Yes, sir. As for your flight, shall I book you on the next available one out of Iloilo?"

He took a deep breath, taking a few seconds to look at Koreen next to him. Her cat-like eyes were now wide open, watching him closely with a mix of hope and trepidation.

"Sir?" Yoshida's voice broke through his trance.

"I'll let you know what's going to happen next, Kotaro-san," Royce replied in Nihongo. "I may need to take that vacation, after all."

"Of course, sir."

"Stay safe. Thank you."

Yoshida murmured a welcome before hanging up.

"What happened?" Koreen asked after he'd put the phone away.

He took her chin into his hand. "My flight's been canceled because of the storm. I'm not going anywhere today. I don't think I'm going anywhere for a few days, at least."

A smile broke across her face, more radiant than any sunrise. "I don't think I'm going anywhere for a few days, either."

He chuckled, nuzzling her neck, kissing his way down to her breasts. "Sounds about right."

"We've been so stupid, you know," she said softly, even as her body eagerly responded to his touch.

Curious, he looked up at her. "What makes you say that?"

"From the beginning, everything was telling us we were meant to be together—getting paired up in Karate, how we both did so well in school, our failed relationships, these storms."

He listened closely, allowing her words to wash over him. By the time she mentioned the weather, he was grinning, his lips seeking her nipples. "No complaints from me."

"I'm serious, Royce. How many storms have to happen before we realize that?"

"I'm serious, too. I was the one who wanted to get married, remember?"

She huffed in frustration. "That's not even what I meant, but you're right. Why do you always have to one-up me in everything?"

"Because I love you. Because that's what we're meant to do to each other." As soon as he was done speaking, he dove right back into her, kissing and licking her nipples until they were rock-hard.

"Royce Duran—"

He didn't let her finish. His hand had sneaked its way into her folds, causing her to squeal in surprise.

"Stay with me, my queen," he said, moving his fingers in and out of her, using his palm to tease her nub. "Stay with me until this storm is over."

Nothing more was said as he moved between her legs, teasing her entrance with his arousal before he entered her. He brought her legs high and wide, driving into her wetness until their moans filled the room.

Sated, they lay back on the pillows, still breathless from their release.

Even in their blissful post-coital state, Koreen Cisco

asserted her supremacy. Even in love, she knew how to one-up him, too.

"I don't want to stay until this storm is over," she said, her voice muffled by his skin as she pressed against his chest. "I want to stay until the next, and the one after it. I go all or nothing, remember?"

He nodded, wrapping his arms around her. "I like the sound of that."

"What about this?" With one quick movement, she was on top of him. "Do you like the sound of this, too?"

She reached for his hardness and sank onto it, glorious and sure in her movements as she rode him, grinding and bouncing, to a tidal wave of ecstasy.

And, yes, he did like the sounds they both made.

As they finally lay next to each other, drifting off to sleep, legs entwined, he reached out to touch her. As he ran his fingers through her hair and down her cheek, she reached out, too, her hand landing on the spot where his heart was, ever only beating for her.

"I love you, Koreen," he told her.

Her eyes drifted open, a smile forming on her lips as she replied, "I love you, too." Moments later, she was fast asleep, her hand still firmly in place.

It was then that he realized that the gap between them had never truly been a wall.

It was a bridge, one they had been too afraid to cross. All they really needed to do was reach out to each other.

With their fear gone, replaced by love, they had finally found their way, closing the last divide between their hearts.

EPILOGUE

Koreen

CROSSED

It was the end of another week—and she looked forward to the next.

Koreen watched her students gather their laptops and tablets, smiling as she listened to their enthusiastic chatter about job interviews and weekend plans with friends, acknowledging and responding as they bid her goodbye.

Once everyone had left, she took a moment to draw a deep breath and look around the classroom, making sure everything was ready for tomorrow's longer, more intensive weekend sessions. She was making her way out when she was met at the threshold by a trio of girls from her old BPO training center. They had followed her when she'd opened her own facility months ago.

"Miss Koreen!" Althea exclaimed, bouncing on her toes with excitement. "You have a visitor waiting in your office!"

"Really? This late?" It was closing time; her session had been the last one for the day.

"Trust us, you'll want to see him." Jane giggled, nudging her friend knowingly.

"Alright, alright." Koreen shook her head in amusement. It was probably the security guard who went around the building before his night shift, selling something his wife had made, usually rice cakes, to the tenants.

She began to walk towards the door, but before she could leave the room, the girls descended on her like a pack of eager stylists. They straightened her clothes, spritzed her lightly with cologne, and applied powder and lip gloss.

"Good?" Someone took out her hair from its ponytail, fluffing up the locks to fall over her shoulders.

The other two girls standing in front of Koreen nodded seriously, like a panel of judges.

"With the amount of time we were given, we did excellent," May, the group's *de facto* leader, said approvingly.

"Okay, that's enough," Koreen laughed, gently pushing them away. "Thank you, girls. You should be going home now. Don't forget, we have skills assessments on Monday. Good night."

After waving goodbye to the girls from the small hallway as they exited the center, Koreen headed to her office.

Her office.

The thought always made her feel a swell of pride at what she had accomplished. What once had been a dream was now a reality; her small business was thriving. Located in a cozy office building adjacent to the almost completed Boundless

Tower, it may have been tiny—with only three classrooms, a reception area, a staff room, and her office—but it was successful. Most importantly, it was hers.

Named Unison, her facility operated on a unique business model. Their training programs were bespoke to the needs of partner corporations. Her students, trained on specific required skill sets, with a syllabus approved and subsidized by each hiring company, were funneled into Boundless and other call and transcription centers. Most of the time, they would quickly be placed in supervisory positions. In her new space, she was able to cultivate a new generation of leaders.

As she reached for the doorknob, she smiled at the modest nameplate before her.

KOREEN T. CISCO
Owner/Manager
UNISON TRAINING & PLACEMENT

"Good eve—" The words caught in her throat as soon as she laid eyes on her 'visitor.'

Seated on one of the small chairs facing her desk, idly perusing brochures, was Royce.

He looked up when she entered, a mischievous glint in his eyes.

"Hey there," he said casually, as if it were perfectly normal for him to be sitting in her office halfway across the world from where he was supposed to be. "I really like what you've done with the place."

"What are you doing here?" Heat suffused her cheeks and stomach at the sight of him only a few feet away.

"I'm here to see my girlfriend," he replied with a smirk,

clearly enjoying her surprise. "Besides, a partner can check on his business anytime, right?"

"Yeah, you can," she grudgingly admitted. He did own half the business as the one who had provided the capital and corporate contacts. "But why didn't you tell me you were coming home?"

"Where's the fun in that?" He grinned, standing up and closing the distance between them.

Koreen couldn't help herself; she practically leaped into his arms the moment he was within reach. Their lips met in a passionate, explosive kiss—from months upon months of pent-up longing and desire. All propriety vanished as Royce reached over to lock the office door, his fingers deftly sliding the bolt.

As they continued to devour each other, he cleared her desk with a single, powerful sweep of his arm and lifted her onto it with a growl. They fumbled with buttons and zippers, pushing enough of their clothes aside to allow their bodies to join together.

"God, I've missed you so much," he groaned into her ear as he drove into her with a force enough to break the table she was on. She welcomed every thrust and lick and kiss, meeting each with equal fervor.

"I've missed you too," she panted. "I love you so much."

With one last suckle on a partially exposed breast, he turned her over. Bending her body over the desk, he lifted her skirt and pushed her legs apart.

"I missed this," he murmured as he reached from behind to tease her opening with his fingers. "I dreamt of doing this to you every single fucking night."

She gasped when he entered her, the sensation of being stretched and filled making her heady.

"Then what are you waiting for?" she breathed, feeling his hands tighten on her hips.

He didn't answer, but instead began to move inside her.

It was heavenly; she could barely hold on to the edge of the table as he pushed her to the brink and, with a final shout of her name, followed closely behind.

He collapsed on top of her. She could feel him shaking from his climax, feel his warm release dripping down her leg.

"I love you," he said, nuzzling her hair and the back of her neck. "I'm so glad to be home."

As the last echoes of their passion faded, he helped her up and they quickly dressed in silence. Decent once more, he pulled her into his arms for a chaste kiss on the forehead. "Ready to head out?"

Koreen nodded. Together, they locked up the training center and made their way to the outdoor car park. As they stepped into the cool night air, she glanced at the glittering Boundless Tower in the distance. It had become her habit over the past few months; the sight of the magnificent building made her feel closer to him.

Royce noticed her gaze and put his arm around her shoulders, pausing to look at the Tower himself.

"She's ours now," he declared.

"Ours?"

"Boundless Tower," he clarified without hesitation. "Or what used to be."

"What do you mean, used to be?" She looked at him and the building, and back again.

Even with the limited lighting in the car park, she could

see the grin on his face. "I bought out Boundless Tower from Prince Khalid, Koreen. I asked him if he was willing to sell it and he agreed, on the condition that I make him a foreign partner in the business."

She stared at him, slowly processing his words. She reached for his hand and gripped it tightly.

"I quit my job in Saudi," Royce said, his smile widening. "I'm not the CEO of Boundless Telecommunications anymore. That's why I'm back...I came home."

"Really?" Her heart thundered in her ears at the realization that he was staying—with her, for good.

He nodded. "I wanted to come home to you...so here I am. Surprise."

With a cry, she launched herself into his arms, sending her bags crashing to the pavement. Their lips met again and again, as she laughed and cried in his embrace.

"I'm going to rename the business, too, and the Tower, of course," Royce said, setting her down gently back on her feet and wiping her tears away with his thumb.

"Rename it? To what?"

"Crown. Fit for a queen."

Koreen felt a blush rise to her cheeks. "I like it. No, I love it."

The happiness on his face was unmistakable as he spoke. "I knew you would. You gave me the idea when I first invested in your training facility. I thought it was brilliant; to have a business of your own, no matter how small. I took a page out of your book, Koreen—I didn't want to be an employee forever, either. I wanted my own place to belong to."

She hugged him tightly around the torso. "You belong with me."

"Exactly." His arms went around her shoulders as he pressed kisses to her hair. "So, where to next?"

"Wherever you want to go, as long as we're together."

He smiled slyly. "Good, because I'm staying at my old room. I thought you'd want to go there for dinner."

She laughed, but the meaning behind his words made her shiver in anticipation. Yes, she would have dinner, and then she would have him.

"I miss that room," she admitted.

He kissed her nose lightly before he let go to pick up her scattered belongings. Hand in hand, they walked to her car.

Upon arriving at the hotel, she was surprised to see him practically leap out of the passenger seat, offering his hand with an infectious grin. She took it, giggling at his enthusiasm.

"Royce, slow down, we haven't even eaten yet," she teased, though she found herself matching his pace, moving through the familiar halls a little breathlessly.

"I have something better planned. Something very special."

He hoisted her into his arms as soon as they exited the elevator at the penthouse level. He didn't let her go until they were inside the suite.

Hands on her waist, he steered her in the direction of the bedroom. Her breath caught as she spotted a single white anemone, partially wrapped in black paper and tied with colorful ribbons, sitting in the middle of the giant bed.

She turned to him, unable to read the expression on his face. She'd given him the dried petals all those months ago… Her vision wavered and blurred and, suddenly, she was sixteen years old again.

She was on a storm-ravaged football field, unable to say

anything—not even goodbye—to the boy who owned her heart.

"Koreen?"

Royce's voice broke through to her in the present, sixteen years on. She turned to the sound and there he was, tall and strong, sure and steady, next to her.

"Can you please get that for me?" He inclined his head towards the lone flower, a small smile on his lips.

Without a word, she stepped forward and carefully picked up the anemone. As she did so, something cold and hard slid into her palm.

Startled, she opened her hand to reveal a gleaming platinum-white ring. It was adorned with a square-cut black jewel.

"It's a diamond." His voice was hoarse and shaky.

When she turned to look at him again, he was on bended knee, his head lowered.

"Royce..." She reached out with her free hand, running her fingers through his hair, smoothing the beard she had grown to love so much on him.

He put his hand over hers, his gaze slowly moving up to her face. "I couldn't find a cardboard box this time around. But I thought...maybe this would be a suitable replacement."

Tears pricked at the corners of her eyes as the full weight of his gesture hit her.

This time, I will listen.

I will let him know how I feel, too.

This time, she wasn't afraid anymore.

She crossed the last few inches that separated them, never taking her eyes off him as he slid the ring onto her finger.

"It is," she said. "Yes, it is."

ANGEL

PLAYLIST

"My Heart"
Paramore

"Secret Love Song"
Little Mix & Jason Derulo

"Dusk till Dawn"
Zayn & Sia

"Going Under"
Evanescence

"Hero"
Enrique Iglesias

"Put Your Arms Around Me"
Texas

ONE

STRANGER

She gazed at the sky for probably the umpteenth time in the past hour.

It was a starry night. The North Star and the many known constellations stood out clearly, brightly. The moon was bright and perfectly spherical. There was no chance of rain.

It was the kind of night for romance, at least for a teen-aged girl.

Stella Montero sat by herself at the street corner. The bench, with a newly dried coat of fresh paint, courtesy of a congressman, was right by the bus stop.

This was her favorite intersection, one she had grown up in. It was always brightly-lit by traffic lights and neon storefront signs. Green, red, orange, yellow and blue; it was its own kind of rainbow.

A gust of wind blew, stirring the street before her.

Discarded newspapers and fliers flew by, tumbling on the stone pavement decorated by graffiti as colorful as the lights overhead.

Stella looked at the sky again. In mere seconds, it seemed to have grown murky and cloudy, as if someone had stolen the lights.

The stars were not the only ones that disappeared that night. Her hopes had gone, too.

Was it only this afternoon when Aaron called and asked if she wanted to go to the movies with him? Was it only a few hours ago when she, drifting on fluffy white clouds, had put on her best dress and favorite shoes and snuck into her mother's room to use her makeup and perfume?

She had already fallen from those clouds. More like stumbled, fell, and landed on the cold hard ground on her ass.

Six-thirty, the time she was supposed to meet Aaron Soler, had come and gone.

It was getting cold. She looked at her watch. It was already half past eight. She pulled her now-rumpled white cardigan more tightly around her body, shoving her hands into their shallow pockets. She would be an idiot if she allowed herself any more hope that he would show up at all. She had more self-respect than that.

"Stood you up, hasn't he?" The voice came out of nowhere, causing her to nearly jump out of her skin.

She sprang to her feet and backed a few feet away, hands clenching into fists as she turned to face the owner of the voice.

She had a box cutter in her bag, she thought, comforted. A girl who grew up in a city like hers knew how to protect herself.

He emerged from underneath the awning of an ice cream shop.

It was a boy. No, a man, tall and dangerous-looking as any predator of the shadows.

He had a thick mane of hair that fell past his shoulders. His skin was duskier than most, allowing him to blend easier into the night. Most of his face was still shrouded in the darkness; what she could see was about a third of his profile, sharp and harsh.

He was the most fearsome and compelling sight she had ever laid eyes on.

"Who are you?" It was almost a shriek, nothing like her own voice. "What do you want?"

He advanced into the light. His face looked even harder and older. There was a scar that ran the length of his right cheek, hidden in part by his long hair. He appeared to be in his early twenties, perhaps older.

"My name is Trey," he said, almost formally. "Hello, Stella."

She backed further away, hot and cold rushing through her veins at the same time.

"How did you know my name?" she demanded.

He gave a slight shrug, his shoulders rippling. "I asked."

She drew herself to her full height of five-foot-five, enough to intimidate most boys her age. It would probably have no effect on him, seeing that he was much bigger, but there was no harm in trying to appear braver than she actually was. "Asked who?"

"The people here. Everyone knows you."

"The people?" she echoed, stumped.

"You see them every day."

She stared, trying to understand what he meant.

Them? The people?

She blinked, slightly taken aback by the bright light coming out of the open doorway of the leather repair shop down the street. She shut her eyes for the briefest of moments. When she opened them, she saw the sweet old woman who ran the shop give her a smile and a friendly wave. Seconds later, someone else left the shop, the old man who did all the repairs by hand or using an ancient pedal machine.

She watched them lock up the shop and walk off.

She understood.

This was her intersection, her neighborhood, her city.

"Yes," she said, more to herself than to the stranger. "I see them every day."

"So you do."

She glared up at him, feeling infinitely more confident that she did minutes ago. "That doesn't explain why you're here, or what you want from me."

"With you? Nothing." Trey sat on the bench she had vacated, draping his arm over the back of the seat and extending his legs. With his dark shirt and jeans, he looked like a giant snake, coiled and poised to strike. "Why I'm here has everything to do with your friend, the pretty boy."

"Aaron?"

"We were tipped off by one of his sidekicks. They come here and pick up girls for their pot sessions. The last one didn't go so well. Joshua didn't want to be part of the repeat performance."

'Pretty boy' Aaron, who was supposed to be her date, was a senior and the most popular boy at their college. His father was the mayor of one of the smaller towns that bordered the city. Aaron always had a lot of boys in his entourage, mostly those from more affluent families; they moved around the school as if they owned it. Girls who got his attention instantly became the most popular ones at school. With her being only a freshman, his initial attentions had flattered Stella to no end.

"Joshua." She repeated the name, trying to jog her memory. "He's the one with the red car. He was supposed to pick me up tonight, with Aaron, and…" Her voice trailed off.

"Joshua Benitez won't be coming, either," he said. "As for Aaron Soler, let's just say his plans have changed."

Girls. Pot sessions. Repeat performance. His words kept echoing in her head as she stood stock-still on the sidewalk. This time, she shivered for real. The night breeze was nothing compared to the cold coming from within her

"Did you want to sit down?" Trey moved his arm out of the way and slid to one side of the bench.

Stella hurried over and plopped down next to him, before she collapsed from the sheer weight of information she was absorbing.

"How long has this…been going on?" So many questions popped into her head, but it was difficult to put them into words. This was the kind of urban cautionary tale picked up and sensationalized by late-night crime investigation shows. "How did you know about them? How the hell do I know you're even telling the truth?"

"I don't have to answer any of that, do I?" He leaned forward, placing his elbows on his thighs and clasping his massive hands between them. He turned his head and peered at her face. "Or would you really want me to?"

She found herself looking into his eyes. They were

midnight-black, unblinking. Strangely, she felt no discomfort under his gaze; instead, she stared right back.

"I just wanted to go on a date with Aaron, you know," she said softly. "When he asked me out, I was on top of the world, everyone at school was looking at me. They all saw me. And Aaron…he actually knew who I was, he got my name right and everything."

"I'm sure he did." There was no sympathy or sarcasm in his voice. He sounded as if he didn't have to convince anyone of anything. "He knew Victoria, Yasmeen, Jennifer and Grace very well, too. Unlike you, they never stood a chance."

Stella didn't know the other three, but Jennifer Ang was a sophomore Aaron had dated the previous semester. She was a beauty queen, slated to compete in the national circuit of pageants that coming summer. Shortly after Jennifer and Aaron broke up, Jennifer's parents, who both worked abroad, had pulled her out of college in the middle of the year and brought her with them to Singapore. There had been rumors of a pregnancy, a party blunder that displeased her sponsors and ruined her image, an expulsion notice that was kept quiet…

"I knew Jennifer," she said. "She's a beauty queen who used to go to my college. She was his girlfriend for a while. She left town end of last semester."

"She got lucky. Grace was from about six weeks ago; she was studying Political Science in the university across town. She sat where you are sitting now. They saw her here before she got in the car with Benitez. She's in rehab now."

The strange reality of it all was overwhelming. In a matter of hours, she had been stood up in what was supposed to be the biggest date of life, her great crush had become a junkie who was bad news for girls, and a stranger from out of nowhere had appeared to be some twisted version of a guardian angel.

"Do you know where Aaron is?"

There was a crooked smile at the corner of Trey's mouth. "Do I really have to answer that question? The less you know, the better for you."

"I can't just sit here without knowing anything," she insisted. "If you want me to at least believe in what you're trying to tell me, then give me some answers."

"Soler won't be able to come here tonight. He and his friend are both at the docks. I brought them there earlier. We're trying to get them to sing. If they're lucky, they would get a little beaten down. If not…" He shrugged. "It's not like they even cared about what would happen to those girls."

"And you…you got them there?"

"It's my job. I work for the man who decided to put them there and, at the same time, get you out of something you wouldn't want."

She sat next to him, trying to keep her breathing even. She had somehow stumbled straight into the plot of a cheap action movie. At any other time, this would have felt contrived, even cheesy.

But she felt nothing like that.

This was a close call, not a joke. She could have ended up like any of those girls.

At that moment, Stella wanted nothing more than to see her mother. If anything happened to her, she could not even imagine her mother's reaction, the pain it would cause her. Even thinking about it made her feel *guilty*.

"I think I want to go home," she said.

The intersection was almost empty except for a few

pedestrians and the familiar nighttime vendors who sold peanuts, duck eggs and green mangoes from their baskets. Most of the stores were already closed for the night. She had been there for almost three hours.

"I'll walk you there." He stood up the same time she did. Side by side, she barely made it to his shoulder. "Or wait until you get into a taxi."

"That won't be necessary," she said, flustered. "I live a few blocks away, near the commercial port."

"You can walk on your own if you want. I'll follow, anyway, and make sure you get there."

At any other time, she would have found those words creepy. She would have felt uncomfortable at the very least.

Tonight, however, was the kind of night that brought creepy to shame. If anything, she was past creepy.

With Trey, there was no feeling of discomfort, only a sense of awareness that he was more intimidating than everyone and everything else around her.

"Fine," she said, thinking she would rather have someone like him walking her home, rather than the less impressive assurance provided by her box cutter. "Let's go."

TWO

CRIMINAL

She looked at the sky again, maybe for the seventh time in the past half hour.

It was still raining. It showed no signs of letting up.

Stella stood by the waiting shed next to the main gate of her college. She was still mercifully dry, if not for errant drops of rainwater, brought about by nasty gusts of wind, whipping against her skin and her white college uniform.

This wasn't rain, she thought. This was a full-blown storm, at least Signal Number Two.

Night had been upon them for hours, with clouds blotting out the sun since mid-afternoon. All the classes for the evening finished at seven-thirty. It was already past eight.

The campus would be locked up soon. She would have to brave the storm on foot and wade her way through the flooded streets if she didn't want to get kicked out or get stuck. It was only a matter of time before the water levels got too high, if the rain didn't stop.

It was a simple, straightforward plan. Out the school and through the city's main street, where there was better drainage. She could use the buildings as shelter and sprint the last few hundred meters home past the plaza and the church. She would be soaked to the bone and maybe even get sick, but at least she wouldn't freeze to death outside her own school.

She turned to the other students huddled next to her, looking them over as she took off her shoes. There were three other girls and two boys, all looking as if they had the same predicament as she: brave the rain and flood, or wait it out. Her own choice already decided, she put her shoes in her bag and gave them a silent nod before walking out into the downpour.

It was easy enough to cross the road and make her way past the market. She was able to take shelter in the windows and awnings, up to and until she reached the main street.

By the time she made it to the intersection, the rain was so heavy she could barely see past a few steps in front of her. The shops had closed, with most of their lights and signs put out. What little light there was came from the streetlamps that still worked. She could feel water, cold and sticky, running in quick tiny currents under her feet. Blasted on all sides by strong winds, she could barely stay upright. It was like being in the middle of a sunken, vengeful city.

So much for her plan of using the buildings as shelter. She'd be lucky if she could make it past this junction. One wrong step could lead her into an open drainage hatch, if she didn't fall on her face, drown or get electrocuted first.

She stood in front of the sixty-year-old grocery store,

squinting through the rain at a dim light coming from the window of a single shop across the street.

It was the old couple's leather repair shop. Were they still there? Could she possibly stay with them until this was over? Could she even cover that much ground without dying along the way?

Throwing caution literally to the winds, she drew her bag tighter against her body and sprinted full speed across the darkened road. Her bare feet burned from the roughness of the asphalt and the icy coldness of the flood.

"Hello? Can I please come in?" she called out, half-crashing, half-stumbling against the shop entrance. She pushed the wooden door open with all her strength and promptly ran into a wall.

She felt the wall give way a little, then something grabbed her upper arms, steadying her. It took her a second to figure out that she had run into someone, not something.

"Stella?"

It took a few more seconds for her eyes to adjust to the soft yellowish light inside the shop. Through a haze of stinging rainwater, she could make out a large black figure with equally dark hair and eyes. His face was the last thing that came into focus.

It was him.

"Trey?"

"What the hell are you doing here? Are you okay?"

She flinched at the harshness of his voice, or maybe at the strength of the grip he had on her. She could barely move her upper body.

At least she could still move her head. She nodded. "I'm fine. Can you please let go of me?"

His hands loosened and fell away. She watched him take a step back, inwardly debating with herself whether or not this was all real.

"Did I hurt you?" Without taking his eyes off her, he picked up something from the front counter. It was an emergency lantern, the source of light she had seen through the window. The shadows in the room shifted as he brought the lantern overhead.

"No, it's okay," she replied, a little too aware of how closely they stood to each other. The repair shop had always been tiny, but now it felt considerably cramped and tight. "Where's Auntie Yolly and Uncle Frank?"

"They've gone home. Did you come here to see them? All the shops closed hours ago." There was a note of disbelief in his voice.

She shook her head. "I was going to take shelter here. It was the only place with the lights on. I thought I could get home on foot, but the streets are too badly flooded."

Exhaustion and cold started nipping at her joints. She leaned against the wooden counter and put her bag on top. Her uniform was drenched, the skirt stained by the flood waters.

It was only then that she noticed it.

The blood.

Next to the space where she had put her bag, she spied small streaks of dark red liquid. Her eyes followed the stains over the side, all the way down the floor, to the spot where Auntie Yolly would usually stand to serve customers. Concealed behind the wooden counter were two limp bodies leaning against each other, their faces split open like overripe watermelons.

She screamed.

She tried but never got the chance. He put his arm around her and brought her close to him, pressing her so tightly against his body that any sound she could make was muffled against his chest.

"Stella," he said, very calmly, almost soothingly. "Stella. Stella, look at me. Please don't scream. Just look at me."

She could feel her body shake violently at the gory sight she had just witnessed. She focused on his voice, the welcome heat of his body. She was fine. It was just blood. It wasn't her blood.

"Look at me, Stella," he repeated. "Don't scream. They're not dead. I won't hurt you."

Clutching at his shirt, she willed herself to open her eyes.

She could see, under the light of the lantern he held up, that he was looking at her, too, into her eyes. His own eyes smoldered like hot coals. She focused on them. He wouldn't hurt her.

"Good," he said. "Now breathe."

She breathed out, a long exhale that made her light-headed. She held on to him, kept her eyes locked onto the somehow comforting familiarity of his face, as she tried to get her bearings.

"Please get me out of here," she heard herself say, trying very hard not to think of the bloody pulps next to her.

His face impassive, he let go of her and moved to the entrance to bolt it shut from the inside. When he was done, he gestured for her to go further inside the shop. "Let's go upstairs. If the water gets any higher, we'll be safer there."

Still feeling sick to her stomach, Stella carefully took her bag and did as instructed. Beyond the front of the shop, behind a thin plastic curtain, was the small workroom she was familiar with, lined wall to wall with tools and Uncle Frank's ancient pedal machine. To one side was a narrow flight of steps.

Guided by the light of the lantern, she was able to find her way to the mezzanine in record time. It was no larger than the downstairs area but had a higher ceiling. It appeared to be some kind of storage room for the shop's supplies. At one end of the room was a large glass window.

She put her bag on a shelf and made her way to the window. There was almost nothing to see, except the rain pelting against the glass and a very limited view of the flooded street outside. Most of the working streetlamps she saw earlier had gone out.

"You should sit down." Trey had put down the lamp on a tiny table and was bringing over a wooden stool for her. "You didn't have to see what you just saw. I guess you'd want an explanation?"

She settled on the stool, stretching out her legs and bare feet. She looked at him as he backed up and settled his large frame on the table next to the lamp. He looked bigger than she remembered; his hair was longer, too.

It didn't surprise her that he was talking so casually about the scene downstairs.

"Did you do that to them?" she asked, boldly.

"I did, just before you got here," he answered. "As I said, they're not dead. They're just out. I remember doing the same thing to your old friends a while back."

She remembered that night vividly. After she'd reached home, she had looked over her shoulder to see Trey gone. She had tried not to think about what had happened and had not told anyone, not even her mother. In the Monday that followed, there had been a large ruckus at the college about the two boys and the rest of their circle getting arrested. None of their gang of nine ever made it back to campus. As far as she'd heard, the other boys had been caught in the act of using drugs and hurting girls from other schools. Stella had thought that maybe Joshua had sung a little too well, or maybe Trey and his boss had made him do so.

"What did they do this time? Drugs?" Stella tried not to think of all the blood splattered on the counter and the floor.

"They were going to burn this building down. They got into the shop by breaking the front lock. They probably wanted to make it look like an accident that started from here, with the amount of leather oil they were carrying. They could have easily taken out this entire block, too. These buildings may look like solid stone from the outside, but inside it's all old wood."

"Why would they want to do that?" She thought of all the people who had stores in the block. She had known most of them since she was little; if not by name, she recognized them by face.

"Territory. Those fuckers are not from here, they're not even from Visayas. They're the Zamora family from Manila. They want to control the Pier District, starting with the small businesses. With the livelihood of the people gone, it would be easier to buy them out."

Trey got off the table and walked the length of the room to look out the window himself. "They tried the same thing last month at the port, with the vendor stalls. We barely got there on time. Otherwise, they could have burned down nearly two hundred stalls and parts of the commercial port."

She lived there. Her house was a stone's throw away from those stalls. She used to eat there regularly. "The only thing I heard about the port was that there was a huge riot that broke out among drunks over videoke. It was all over the news last month. My mother warned me not to go there in the evenings once they start all the singing and drinking."

He looked over his shoulder at her. "It was a good story, wasn't it? The boys staged the riot so well and got all the attention. We were lucky at the time."

She hesitated before asking her next question. "What are you going to do about them?" She gestured vaguely downwards.

"We're tracking down their friends who could be in the other buildings. As soon as we could get through the flood, we're taking these sons of bitches to their quarters across town. It took us a while to find out where they're holed up. Turns out they live in the house of Greg Garces. He's got ties with the Filipino-American mafia. I wouldn't be surprised if he's the one funding this little takeover attempt."

Another cause, another enemy.

More blood.

Why Trey did what he was doing she had no idea. "What do they want from the Pier District? I've lived here all my life. Most of us in our neighborhood have. It's just boats and warehouses and shops, and tiny old houses like mine."

He turned to face her completely. "Whoever controls the district controls the shipping routes and traffic. What goes in, what goes out, what everybody does in it. Most importantly, who gets to do business. All kinds of business."

"Somebody already does that, right?" She searched her memory for the name. It was a very old name, the elusive but notorious family that owned at least half of the district where she lived. "The Esguerras?"

"Raphael Esguerra. Ever since he took over a few years ago, other families and groups have been trying to take him down on all sides. A new leader usually takes a lot of heat. We've been putting out fires for a while now."

"You do dangerous things" she said. "You could get killed. Can't you just…quit?"

"And do what?"

"I don't know. Live and work somewhere else."

"Some of us can't just quit," he said with more emotion than she'd ever heard. "Some of us can't just give up the life we were born into. I grew up in the docks. I've lived here my whole life, too, just like you. I will do everything in my power to keep the Pier District from getting destroyed by outsiders, even if it means becoming a criminal to get rid of the people in my way."

His eyes left her then, as he focused his attention back to the window.

She stood up and picked her way over to the window, to see what he was looking at. It was still windy and raining heavily.

"I hope it stops raining soon. I want to go home. I've been at school since eight this morning."

"Aren't you cold? You look like you're going to be sick soon." The concern on his face made her aware of their closeness.

All she had to do was reach out, to touch him, to make sure he was real.

Ever since that night at the intersection, she had thought about him constantly, wondering if he ever existed at all. She had wanted to ask others about him, but had decided not to. She knew if he'd been just a figment of her imagination she would be devastated.

She was soaked with rainwater and freezing all the way to her insides. She wasn't even aware she had wrapped her own arms around her body to keep herself warm.

"I'm fine. It was my fault. I forgot my umbrella at the library. By the time I came back to get it, I was too late."

"Here." Trey started unbuttoning his shirt. She stared, heat rushing to her face. She tried to move her legs, to step away from him, but she was frozen to the spot. His black shirt opened, showing a grey t-shirt underneath. He took off the polo and handed it to her. "Put this on."

She was blushing and she knew it. The grey shirt had a tighter fit on his body. His shoulders and chest were broad, contrasting with his flat stomach and narrow hips. His black polo ended up in her shaky hand.

"Thanks," she heard herself choke out.

"I'm sorry if there are any…stains on it. I don't have anything warmer."

His shirt was the warmest thing she had ever touched. It had a clean, fresh scent, something like pine, tinged with the sea. She slid her arms into the shirt, almost disappearing into its considerably larger size.

"It's fine. It's very warm. Thank you."

They both stood by the window in silence, staring out into the rain and the nearly invisible city street.

"How are you, Stella?" It had gotten so quiet, his voice almost startled her. "I didn't get to ask you earlier."

"Life goes on, I suppose," she said. "School has been busier since I was a freshman. Thankfully, no one tried anything since that night. I think everyone got a little bit scared with what happened to Aaron and Joshua."

"A little bit scared?"

"Scared shitless, then?"

"Better."

She smiled. "So, how are you?"

He held up his left hand to the light. His knuckles looked freshly skinned, with a little blood caked and dried on them. "Bloody after my little fun. I guess I'm fine."

She was tempted to reach out and touch his hand. She could only clench her own fingers into a tight fist.

"I don't think I ever got to say thank you," she said.

"For what?"

"For back then." She could feel herself blushing again. She really had to get herself under control. All this caused by someone she barely knew, someone who had the knack of appearing out of the darkness for her, whenever she needed it most. "And for now, I think."

He shook his head. "You're thanking me for showing you two half-dead bodies in a leather repair shop?"

"For being there, Trey. It means something to me, even if the thought had never crossed your mind. Don't be like that."

She was rewarded with the tiniest of smiles. "This is as much of a surprise to me as it is to you, Stella."

The moment was interrupted by his phone ringing. He took it out of his pocket and answered. "Yes. I'm still here. Are you sure there's no one else out there?"

Trey looked out the window again. "Can you drop someone off first, then come back? Good."

"There's a car on the way," he said to her, replacing the

phone in his pocket. "It can get through the flood. They'll take you home."

"That's great. Thanks." She looked around her, never at him. He would disappear again for goodness knew how long. She had to say it. "Will I see you again?"

He was already making his way back to retrieve the lamp from the table. He stopped mid-step and stared at her from over his shoulder. "What?"

"Will I ever get to see you again?" she repeated, as bravely as she could.

"Why would you want to see me? People don't usually like seeing me."

"I like seeing you," she retorted.

"Give me your phone." He walked back to her and held out his hand.

She reached into her bag, between rows of damp notebooks, and retrieved her phone. It was only slightly damp on the outside. The tiny device almost disappeared into his hand.

He looked at her phone's casing for a few seconds. It was made of shiny white silicone, decorated with a stylized drawing of a black archangel. He didn't comment. He turned it over to the screen side and started typing.

She heard his phone ringing again. "That's you calling. I'll save your number. Call me whenever you need, okay? I will answer."

She was tempted to say something in response when he handed the phone back to her. Nothing came out of her mouth. Not even when she retrieved her bag and followed him down the stairs.

She stood as close as she possibly could to the entrance, the farthest from the two bodies behind the counter. Trey was talking on his phone again, to someone else, about meeting them in another district across town.

It barely took any time before the car reached the flooded main street. She saw its headlights approaching and turned to him.

Stella finally found her voice. "Thanks." She took off his shirt and handed it back.

He shook his head. "No, keep it."

"I don't think I can." *Even if she wanted to.* "My mother will ask a lot of questions. It's a very small house. And it's just the two of us."

"Don't worry. I understand." He took the shirt and put it back on just as she heard a muted honking from outside. He unlocked the shop's front door and held it open for her. "Take care of yourself."

"You, too." She walked past him and stepped back into the street. Once outside, she could see that the rain had calmed down. It was still pouring heavily, but she could barely feel the wind.

He followed her. "Tell Mario where you want to go. He'll drive you there."

A dark four-wheel drive had stopped outside the shop. It stood amidst the flood looking like a tank. A middle-aged man rolled down the window by the driver's side and was about to step out when Trey held up a hand and opened the backseat door himself.

"Good night, Stella." The rain dripped on his face and hair. He didn't even blink.

She finally reached out and got to touch his left hand, the one with the skinned knuckles. It felt warm, rough, strong. "Thanks again. Good night."

He nodded and shut the car door. He didn't move from the spot where he stood, not even when the giant car pulled out of the sidewalk and started making its way through the flood.

She never took her eyes off him. Not until the sight of him was swallowed by the darkness that stretched out behind her.

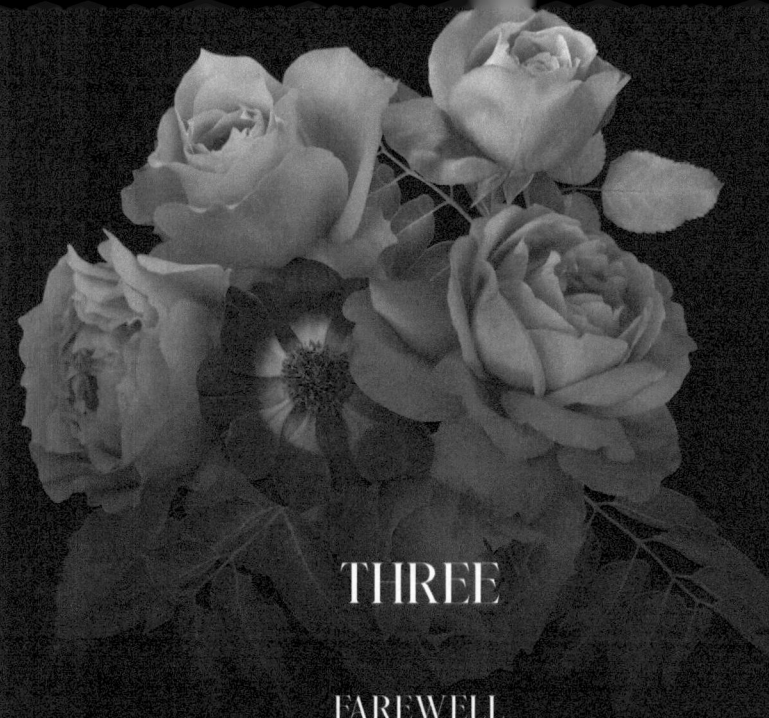

THREE

FAREWELL

She looked up at the sky, then down at her watch. She sighed, trying to find a more comfortable position on the bench. Her legs and feet, clad in the black regulation stockings and low-heeled shoes of her school uniform, felt cramped. She felt warm in the white suit and regretted not changing into something cooler.

In the early evening, the intersection was the same as always, bright, messy and full of people rushing to catch a ride or selling food and trinkets. There was a thick, balmy breeze coming from the nearby waters of the docks, heavily tinged with salt. It was going to be a humid night.

Was it only a few years ago that she had sat on this same bench, shivering in a white cardigan, grappling with the dark realities of the world she was growing up in? It felt like a lifetime ago.

She wasn't surprised when someone suddenly took the spot next to her on the bench. She kind of expected it.

Stella had expected anything to happen since she got the text message from Trey last week. She had never called or messaged him in the past eighteen months since they last saw each other. She had not deleted his number, either.

It was the only message she had ever received from him.

Can we meet

Same place

Friday 6pm

She had called him back straightaway, just to make sure it wasn't someone else messing with her. He had answered after two rings, in that deep, raspy voice that sometimes followed her, especially when she walked alone in the city streets at night. Sometimes she dreamt of that voice, too.

For this Friday, she skipped her last class and told her friends she would meet them at the movies tomorrow evening. She had the foolproof reason of completing a report due that Monday.

"Hi, Stella." Trey, no longer a disembodied presence at the back of her head, looked surprisingly different. His long hair was tied back in a neat ponytail; he was dressed in a green polo shirt, blue jeans and brown shoes. He looked almost normal; his scarred face was as fierce-looking as ever, maybe even a little sharper with age.

Stella wondered how he thought she looked. She had definitely gotten taller since last time. Over the past few years, it was her height that brought her attention and sometimes opportunities neither she nor her mother had ever expected. A few months ago, she was approached by an events company to model for a local fashion show early next year.

"How are you, Trey?" she asked, politely. Light conversation had never been part of their interactions.

His Adam's apple was bobbing up and down. "I'm fine. Thanks for coming. I didn't think you would even answer my text. How have you been?"

She forced a smile, as strange as it felt to have normal small talk with him. "Good. Busy. Reports and exams take up most of my time. I'll be graduating this school year."

There was a rustle as he pulled out something from behind his back. She was certain he had gotten even bigger since last time; his shoulders looked wider in the more flattering cut and color of his shirt.

To her surprise, there was a small box of roses in his hands. There were three: one red, one pink and one white.

"I didn't know which color you liked, but I took a chance and picked roses," he said. "You always have on some kind of cologne that smells like roses."

"Yes, I like roses," she answered, taken aback. "Roses are nice."

If she had to list a hundred things this man was capable of doing, giving her roses would never even be a remote consideration, much less knowing how she actually smelled.

She reached out to take the box, trying to think of something else to say and failing miserably. She wasn't sure if she had intended to touch him, but her hands landed on top of his.

She looked up into his dark eyes and, sure enough, they were on her, too. She understood that look from a man, far better now than she did four years ago. No matter how mysterious he appeared to be, he was still a man, wasn't he?

"I wanted to see you," he finally said, breaking the silent, unmoving exchange between them. "I didn't want to leave town without telling you."

Her fingers closed around the box. It was made of white cardboard, plain yet sturdy, with a plastic display window to showcase the flowers inside. It was something she expected from someone like him: unadorned and straightforward.

"Where are you going?"

"Does it matter?"

"It does to me." She clutched the box closer to her, pressing it to the space between her chest and her stomach.

"I'm going to get a few things out of the way. North, mostly in Manila. We've lost a lot of good people to the Zamoras this past year. They haven't stopped trying to take over the Pier District."

His back heaved in what looked like a sigh. "It's only a matter of time before this escalates to an all-out war. But Iloilo is our home, we were born and raised here. We won't give it up, so we're bringing the war to them."

He was bringing the war to them, she thought.

Stella suddenly felt cold, empty, abandoned. The same way she had felt the first time she met him, on this very bench.

"You'll be back, right? You said before this is the life you were born into. You can't just leave, can you?"

There was that familiar tiny smile at the corner of his mouth. "It's not about leaving or staying. When I chose to do this, I knew I wouldn't be coming back. Sometimes, there are things we need to do that we can't just walk away from."

"I see," she said, evenly. "You'll be missing my graduation, then." It sounded stupid and pointless, but nothing ever made sense with him anyway. She could not even fathom how deep, dark and bloody the world he lived in was.

"I guess I will."

"I was a freshman when we first met, you know."

He nodded. "So, are you going to the senior prom with someone special?"

"Prom?" she echoed. "I haven't really thought about it. I don't have a special someone."

The idea had never really crossed her mind, not since what happened during freshman year. She had nothing against boys in general, but since then she had been averse to the young adult rituals of courting and dating.

Sure, there were a few boys who showed interest, some more than others. Darryl, whose family moved from another province at the start of their junior year, had been courting her shortly after he completed his first semester at the college. He was part of the student council and tutored younger students in Math subjects. Her mother liked him immensely. Stella didn't exactly dislike him; she just wasn't interested.

"It took me a while to trust boys again, after what happened. But I've learned a thing or two since then. I would stick an idiot in the throat with a box cutter before they could try anything funny." She had to smile through the heaviness in her muscles, a strange sensation considering how empty she felt inside.

They sat in silence for a while, before he stood up.

"I'm glad you're okay, Stella. At least I got one thing right in all of this."

Driven by a sudden sense of panic, she jumped to her own feet. "Are you going now?" she blurted out.

"I'm leaving tomorrow morning, so I'd better get ready."

He was looking down at her with his mouth in a thin line. "I'm sorry if I bothered or upset you in any way. If there was someone I had to say goodbye to, it was you."

She felt something rise in her throat, bitter and painful and stinging hot.

Goodbye, she thought. It sounded so final and absolute.

Guardian angels were supposed to stay, weren't they? Wasn't he supposed to stay with her?

"I'm glad you told me," she said honestly. "It gave me a chance to see you. I thought I'd see you again sooner, after last time. But I'm glad you're here now."

"Me, too."

She swallowed hard, trying her best to stem the flood rising dangerously fast from within her. "It's early. I skipped my last class to meet you."

Before he could respond, she continued. "Let's eat something, okay? It will be my treat. I never had the chance to do anything for you."

Without giving him the opportunity to refuse, she grabbed him by the arm and pulled him through the throng of people milling the busy nighttime streets. She knew this place was part of him. This was home for Trey.

They had dinner of grilled fish and rice at a small, open-air eatery on the docks. It was nice to see him doing something normal with her, for a change.

Or for the last time.

It was almost nine in the evening when the lights of the stores and restaurants started going out, signaling the end of the day. She thought back to the time she had sat at the intersection and looked at the dying stars as her own hopes died, too.

Trey was the only constant presence between then and now, between an innocent teenager's disappointment and her first real heartbreak.

Her twisted kind of guardian angel, who was leaving her life as soon as the day was over. She was determined not to lose any more time she had left with this beguiling man.

"You live near here, don't you?" She had her hand on his arm, a gesture she had dared to try earlier, as they walked on the open pier, the area where smaller passenger boats docked in the daytime. She had thought he would not want to be touched, but she was wrong. She was glad to be wrong.

"It's near the old Customs office," he said, a little too formally, nodding towards a cluster of warehouses a block away. "My boss bought a few buildings here to keep some of the cars and for us to stay in if we wanted. I didn't want to live out of town."

"Can I see your place?" Heat flooded her face at her own boldness.

He stopped in his tracks. "It's late. I should be walking you home."

"I don't want to go home. Not yet."

"What do you want, then, Stella?"

Before her mind realized what she was doing, her body and heart had already made the call.

Her school bag, with his gift of roses, slid off her shoulder as she let go of his arm to, finally, put her own arms around him. She could reach his shoulders, his neck; she had to stand on tiptoes and force his head down with all her might. And it worked.

She kissed him.

FOUR

RECKONING

She didn't think about it anymore. She just moved as she had always wanted to. She ran her hands over his back and his thick hair; she used her tongue to taste him, his lips, the inside of his mouth. The rest of her followed; her chest and her hips pressed against him, wanting more, maybe at least for him to touch her, too.

He understood.

She knew as much when he came to life, knowing exactly what she wanted, what she needed.

His lips moved against hers; his tongue was deliciously soft and snake-like as it twisted its way into the depths of her mouth. His hands were all over her. His fingers ran through her long hair, his palms burned a path through her skin as he wrapped his arms around her waist and started caressing her buttocks. It wasn't very long until she was pressed against him so tightly, she could feel him, hard and insistent, against her own softness. His fingertips glided inside her skirt as he lifted one of her legs to wrap around his hip.

She gasped when he touched that part of her, expertly reaching inside the modest underwear she wore with her school uniform. His fingers rubbed and stroked her as she moaned against his chest.

She denied herself the pleasure that was beginning to build and decided to come back up for air. She grabbed at his arms, still feeling him against her.

"Take me home, Trey," she whispered into the night. "Make me yours."

He was always more at ease in the shadows. She watched as he picked up her things with ruthless efficiency. This time, it was his turn to take her hand and lead the way.

He lived in a warehouse, one filled with auto parts. The lighting was sparse; except for a few fluorescent bulbs, it was the lights of the pier that danced with the shadows. He locked the door behind him and led her to a tiny corner where stood a small table, a portable chest of plastic drawers, a tiny refrigerator, and his bed, wooden, with a thin mattress on top.

He did not say anything; neither did she. He brought her to the bed and made her stand before him. He undressed her then, unbuttoning her blouse and skirt first and sliding them off of her. He fumbled a bit with her bra, but when he finally undid the clasp and took it off, she blushed deeply as he brought his lips to her nipples and suckled them hungrily. She would have fallen to the floor, easily, had it not been for his firm grip around her body.

When he was done, he lowered her stockings and panties and, before she could protest, his lips, his tongue and his hands were on her, all over her. After a few moments, he lifted her to the bed, settling her gently on her back. His mouth came down between her legs again, as did his fingers, and she was at his mercy. She called his name, bucked her hips, spread herself further, dug her nails into his shoulders, until he brought her to the peak and she heard herself scream and moan in pleasure.

"You are so beautiful." She heard him speak huskily, from somewhere above her. It took a few seconds for her eyes to focus as she came down from what she knew was her first climax. She had read about it in romance novels, seen it in movies that made her blush, and even heard girls with boyfriends talk about it, but she had never expected it to feel like this.

She had never expected she would feel it with him.

In what little light there was, she could see him next to her on the bed, his dark eyes almost disappearing into the shadows. He was still fully clothed.

"Oh." Embarrassment sank in for the first time. Her hands came up, to cover her utter lack of modesty, but his fingertips were on her face before she could reach for something, like a blanket or pillow, to cover up with.

"You don't have to hide. Never from me." For the first time, she heard a tremble in his voice. She could barely see his face. His fingertips were gentle as he traced her cheeks; the skin on his hands was hard, rough and warm. She could smell herself in his touch.

She reached for him. Before she could wrap her arms around him again, he caught her wrists.

"I think it's time for you to go home." There it was again, the shakiness in his voice. "I'll walk you there." He slowly let her go.

"No," she said, trying to lift her torso, to get a better look at him. "I want to stay with you."

He hesitated, then sat up, the cot creaking under his weight. "This is your…first time, isn't it?"

"Yes." Was there something she had done he didn't like? "What does that have to do with anything?"

"This is the biggest mistake you could ever make." His back was as stiff and unyielding as a mountain, his voice low and almost menacing.

"Mistake? Who made you responsible for my decisions?" Heat rushed to her cheeks and forehead. She grabbed at the thin striped blanket folded under the pillow she had been lying on and hastily wrapped it around her nakedness.

"Decision? You call this a decision? To sleep with me?"

"To be with you, Trey." She was close to tears. She slid off the bed and got to her feet. He still had his back turned to her. At least he couldn't see her so disheveled and hurt. "I want to be with you. It was my choice to make. Don't you dare tell me you didn't want it, too. I felt it. Don't you fucking dare deny it."

He put his hands on his thick legs and rose, almost painstakingly. "I'm not denying anything." He turned slowly, running his fingers through his hair, which had become half-unbound after their kisses. He kept his eyes hooded, gaze to the floor, or at least not on her.

"I've never wanted a woman as much as I want you. Look at you, Stella. How could I or any man say no to you?"

"Then don't."

"If only it were that simple. If only I were any other man."

"You will never be any other man," she said, almost impatiently. "Look at you, Trey. How could any man compare to you?"

"Any other man wouldn't leave you." It was almost a whisper.

That stopped her.

"Then come back." Her lips finally uttered the very thing her heart had known for a long time. "When all this is over, come back to me."

As soon as she finished saying the words, a lone tear slid down the corner of her left eye, landing and splashing on her naked shoulder. She was terrified he saw it.

That was the last shred of her dignity.

Somehow, that was also the last shred of his control.

As long as it took her to blink back more tears, he closed the distance between them. The way he grabbed hold of her around the waist was almost bone-breaking, crushing the breath out of her. His lips came down on hers like a clap of thunder, as powerful and overwhelming as he.

Her flimsy cover of a blanket fell to the floor, just as she gave him her complete surrender. This time, there was no waiting, no caressing, no gentleness, as she kissed him back like a woman starved.

Dimly, she felt her hands rip away at the last barriers between them, his clothing. It didn't take long for him to be just as naked as she. He looked beautifully inhuman in the dim light and shifting shadows; his skin was smooth where there were no scars, but he had dozens of them all over his body, mixed with what looked and felt like burn marks. His hair fell on her face like a velvet curtain, scented by the sea and his sweat.

They didn't even make it to the bed, or at least she did, halfway. He was inside her, a perfect fit, buried completely, as her legs went around his waist, his shadow looming over her. She felt him thrusting faster and harder by the second, heard him say her name again and again, and, finally, asked her to look at him.

Their eyes locked briefly, and she drowned at the ferocity and desire she saw in the way he looked at her, and his lips were on hers again. He thrust the hardest then, and he shouted as his body shook as if he had a hundred earthquakes inside him, from inside her.

He collapsed, draped across her, his hair and sweat and breath on her breasts. She could feel a slick wetness burning straight from him into her.

Her heart was pounding so loudly she could barely hear anything else. She put her arms around him and kissed the top of his head, feeling only tenderness as she watched him looking spent and vulnerable.

Is this how it was supposed to feel?

She never had any more time to think about it that night. She could only feel, only him. They made love again, and again, and once more. He was insatiable, as if he wanted every last part of her for himself, but, to her surprise, so was she.

By dawn, he had touched and kissed every inch of her, and she of him. She was straddling him, arms around his neck, his teeth and tongue on her nipples, when she saw the first strains of light filter in through the high windows of the warehouse. By the time she came in his embrace, moaning his name, morning was upon them.

He was on his back and she sprawled on top of him, nuzzling his chest, when she realized it was the first time she was seeing him in the light of day.

"Come back to me, Trey," she blurted out, afraid he would

somehow disappear. "No matter what happens, just come back to me."

He didn't respond, not for a long time. His arms went around her, so tightly, so protectively. She felt his lips on her temple, his heartbeat in her ear, his hands in her hair. She took these in, every touch, every scent, every sound, every feeling.

"I love you, Stella," he finally said.

FIVE

PRISON

I LOVE YOU.
   After he said the words, he slowly moved her to the bed and wrapped her in his blanket. She watched him dress in his usual dark clothing and take only a black backpack.

"It's yours now," he said, giving her the keys he had used the night before. "Do whatever you like."

Before she could protest, he brought his arms around her and kissed her deeply. With one last caress on her cheek and her hair, he was gone.

Trey.

She didn't even know his last name.

Stella got out of his bed, dressed and gathered her things. It was only when she finished locking up the warehouse that she felt the scalding pain in her throat, from last night, finally bubble to the surface, unleashing itself with her tears.

As she walked home, she didn't have the heart to check

her phone, knowing that it was probably bursting with worried texts and missed calls from her mother. She would deal with it all later. All that mattered at the moment was she make it through the pain, see herself home alive.

She had no idea how hard she had been clutching his box of roses in her hands. She was just about to cross the intersection when it fell from her grasp. The box burst open, spilling the three roses onto the street, along with a small rectangle of paper.

She crouched down and slowly gathered the fallen items, fitting them into her school bag, feeling spent and raw as she did. The rectangle turned out to be a business card, with something written on the back of it by hand. The name was familiar.

RAPHAEL I. ESGUERRA, III
Chief Executive Officer
Esguerra Holdings

Trey's boss. There was a number printed underneath, which looked oddly familiar. It took her a few seconds to figure out that the mobile phone number was Trey's. She had looked at his number and only message from last week so many times.

Why was his phone number on his boss' card?

At the back of the paper, in bold, slashing handwriting, was a short message.

Call whenever you need.

There will be an answer.

Trey

Unable to make sense of what she had just read, she

fumbled with the rest of her things and slowly sat down at the bench by the intersection, taking deep breaths.

She slowly went back in memory, to what he had said in the time she was with him.

"Iloilo is our home, we were born and raised here. We won't give it up, so we're bringing the war to them."

"I work for the man who decided to put them there and, at the same time, get you out of something you wouldn't want."

"When I chose to do this, I knew I wouldn't be coming back."

"Some of us can't just quit. Some of us can't just give up the life we were born into."

Was Trey the boss he was referring to? Was he actually Raphael Esguerra?

Was he the Raphael Esguerra who protected her city?

Unable to stop herself, she took out her phone. The screen showed eighteen missed calls and almost double in unread messages. The battery was down to twelve percent. She scrolled through her contacts, found Trey's number, and called it. She felt an icy chill envelop her body, despite the warmth of the morning sun.

Her call was picked up after two rings.

"Hello, Miss Montero. Good morning." The voice was different, older, female. It sounded almost like her own mother's voice.

"Hello," Stella echoed. She suddenly felt disoriented. "Who's this? Is Trey there?"

"My name is Rhoda, Miss Montero. I work for Mister Esguerra. Is there something I can do for you?"

"Where's Trey? I want to talk to him. Please."

"I believe he has informed you he will be indisposed. He

has given us instructions to be at your service, as and when you need."

Us? Her brain tried to cope with the words of the woman at the other end of the line. *At her service?*

Wherever Trey was, she had already gotten her answer.

"No, thanks," she heard herself say. "I just wanted to give him back the keys to his... house."

"Did you? I was under the impression he has given them to you, to access and use the warehouse as you please."

"No. Yes. I didn't understand what he was trying to tell me."

There was a pause from Rhoda. "Is there anything else you need, Miss Montero? I can send a car for you if you need to get somewhere, wherever you are in the city."

To her horror, Stella felt a few tears slowly escape her already stinging, sleepless eyes. "I don't need a car. I'll walk home."

"Very well, Miss Montero. Please call me if you need anything, anything at all."

"Goodbye, Rhoda." Stella disconnected the call. She mechanically picked up her bag and stood up. She could feel her legs extend unwillingly, still sore from her night with him. She was beyond tired.

Raphael Esguerra.

A powerful name, feared and respected in the world she lived in.

Trey.

The man who moved in and out of the shadows and into her life, into her darkest dreams and desires.

They were the same person. The only man she had given her heart and her body to.

She would have given anything to make him stay. She knew, however, that no one could tell someone like Raphael Esguerra what to do.

The very same person who told her he loved her.

She had never said she loved him, too, had she? Loved him the moment she first laid eyes on him all those years ago, stepping out of the darkness, under the bright neon lights of a street corner.

It was the only regret she had. It was a prison she willingly put her heart into.

She carried this regret in the days, weeks and months that followed, silently, guardedly.

When she reached home that Saturday morning, instead of greeting her with panic or anger, her mother told her that she received a visitor named Rhoda, the mother of one of Stella's classmates, earlier that morning. Rhoda had apologized for not calling to tell her that Stella was helping her daughter with an urgent term paper, help given at the last minute to a desperate classmate. After breakfast in a fast food restaurant with her daughter, Stella would be home.

She went to the movies that evening with her friends. On Monday, the student council started putting up posters for the senior prom, scheduled on Valentine's Day. She wasn't surprised to get asked by Darryl, whom she politely turned down. In the weeks that followed, she refused four more invitations.

It was almost Christmas when she first heard about it on the news.

It was hard to miss. A large explosion in Sampaloc, Manila had taken down almost four blocks of factories and warehouses. A hundred injured, twenty dead. Up to and until Christmas, there were interviews of a bereaved widow named

Connie Zamora, clutching a brood of four children, mourning the death of her husband, business magnate Michael Zamora. Connie demanded justice for her family and the families of their employees.

The media and the police suspected terrorists trying to make a statement. Stella always looked at the sketches released to the public, but never found one she recognized.

Over the school break that December, just before New Year, she went back to the warehouse, on a quiet weekday evening.

It was the same way she had left it. She tidied up the bed, willing herself not to think of the person she had shared it with, and stripped the sheets for washing. She went through the plastic drawers and the refrigerator. The fridge had a few bottles of water and an unopened Snickers chocolate bar. The drawers contained an assortment of black and grey shirts, a few pairs of dark jeans, and shorts of different colors. All the clothes had been washed and neatly folded. In the bottom drawer was a plain ruled notebook and a few pencils. Nothing was written inside the notebook; there were only sketches that filled the pages, drawn in a neat, meticulous hand.

They were all sketches of her.

She spent the next hour crying on his bare mattress.

In January, she walked the runway for the first time, in a Dinagyang Festival fashion show. The designer was so impressed that she offered to design Stella's gown for the latter's senior prom, as part of her Valentine's Day portfolio.

February came with typhoons, one after the other. The rain on Valentine's Day reminded Stella of that night two years ago when the city was flooded.

The prom was at a seaside resort across town, in a covered

pavilion with tall, thick glass windows that overlooked the beach. In spite of the weather, almost all her classmates and their dates had come.

Stella arrived with two other senior girls who didn't have escorts like her. All three of them lived in the same area and had opted to travel to and from the event together.

She made a stop at the bathroom before entering the venue. Pictures of the night were very important, according to the designer. They had contracted one of the prom photographers to take additional photos of her wearing the new dress.

The gown was made of deep red velvet, the color of blood. The neckline was cut low, off the shoulders, with small crisscrossing straps around her upper arms. The rest of the fabric was molded to her bodice and hips, then came apart by her left thigh in a slit, showing off her long legs, with the hemline almost brushing the floor.

The hairdresser had styled her hair half down, half up. It fell in waves all the way to the middle of her bare back. She had asked for three small roses to be put around the loose ponytail on top of her head. One red, one pink, one white.

'I love you, Stella.'

The words had echoed in her mind, heart and soul countless times since she heard them, for the first, only and, possibly, last time.

Staring back at her in the mirror was the very image of a romantic heroine, draped in the colors of love.

But she wasn't that heroine.

She was Stella Montero, who didn't even have a date to the prom. She didn't have someone special. She already had something more than that.

She already had her prison.

SIX

STORM

The prom was meant to last past midnight. The weather had other plans.

At nearly eleven that evening, Stella stood next to the glass door of the pavilion and looked up. She couldn't see any of the stars. The sky was almost completely covered in thick clouds. There was only the moon, cutting through the dark shroud with tiny yet sharp slivers of light.

The rain fell in a steady downpour, the winds picking up in speed with each hour that passed. A full-blown storm would be upon them soon.

She had spent the past few hours having her picture taken and getting congratulated by practically everyone present: her teachers, classmates and schoolmates, even visitors from other schools. She was, apparently, the frontrunner for Prom Queen.

She was not surprised when someone from the student council came over to escort her across the dance floor. It was the treasurer, a classmate of hers since freshman year named Vic. He guided her up the small stage and led her to a spot in a line where three other girls stood. Vic winked at her and mouthed, *"Congratulations. It's you."*

In one corner of the platform stood the male half of the prom court. Darryl already had the Prom King crown on his head. He was flanked by three other boys from her class who wore blue sashes as the first, second and third princes.

The emcee, a deejay from a popular local radio station, came forward dramatically, brandishing an important-looking cream-colored envelope. He took out a card of the same color and began to read out the names of the third and second princesses.

Stella felt the hug of the last girl standing next to her seconds after she heard her name being called as Prom Queen. The president of the student council came forward and put a pink and gold sash over her shoulder, followed by the college dean who pinned a bejeweled tiara to her hair. She was hugged and kissed by a few more people before Darryl stood in front of her bearing a bouquet of white, yellow and pink flowers, mostly roses. Photographers surged forward and snapped pictures at an alarming, blinding rate.

She could hear the strains of David Pomeranz's song, 'King and Queen of Hearts,' coming over the speakers. This was the traditional Prom King and Queen dance.

The crowd applauded. The catcalls, whistles and whoops were deafening.

The skies responded, splitting open with a resounding, bright burst of lightning. Thunder followed, echoing through the sudden darkness that blanketed the entire pavilion.

"The power just went out," she heard the deejay say loudly. "Everyone please stay calm."

Someone grabbed her hand, pulling her to the left side of the stage. She thought at first it was Darryl, but she was certain he was on the opposite side of the stage, where moments before he stood under the spotlight with an obnoxious-looking bouquet in his hand and a silly grin on his face.

Stella found her voice, her hand instinctively going up to prevent the tiara on her head from falling. She could use it as a weapon, too, just in case.

"What the hell do you think you're doing?" she demanded.

"Hi, Stella." The voice came from the deepest shadows of stage left, the only sound she could hear clearly even with the rising din of people talking in the darkness.

She knew that voice.

"Trey?" she heard herself respond, in what sounded like a desperate whisper. Maybe she had completely lost it now.

Cellphones and lighters began coming to life on the pavilion floor, allowing her to see more clearly.

A single streak of light moved across the spot where she heard his voice coming from, falling on his profile for the briefest moment.

That was all she needed to see.

She unceremoniously pulled the errant tiara off her head and tossed it aside, then jumped off the stage and into his arms.

She landed on his chest, her fingers clutching the fabric of his shirt, her face burrowing into his neck, desperately taking in his familiar scent of pine and the sea.

Trey's hands were warm on her back. He was raining

kisses on her hair and face. She knew the feeling of his lips on her skin.

"Let's get out of here," she heard him say.

Nothing in the world could stop her from going with him. She was not sure if he carried her, or she ran alongside him, but she found herself in a hut at the farthest end of the resort, cloaked by the night and the rain.

Before them, the surf crashed roughly against the shore. Their shelter of dried woven leaves made little consequence. They were both soaked to the skin.

It was only when he stood still before her, in the pale, thin light of the moon, was she finally convinced he was real. She reached out and touched his face, taking in all the planes and angles.

"I missed you so much," she said. "Whoever you are."

"It doesn't matter who I am. It never mattered to you."

He was right. It never did.

"What matters is that I love you." The words came out easily, as naturally as she breathed in the salty air and the heady scent of him. She touched the scar on his right cheek. She watched as he turned his head and started kissing her fingertips.

"You are so beautiful." His voice was equal parts passionate and tender, as was his gaze.

"So are you," she said, as she traced his lips and jawline.

"I came back to you," he said. "Do you know what that means?"

She put her arms around his torso, angling her ear so she could hear his heartbeat. "That you really love me? That you missed me, too?"

"It means I am yours, Stella. I have been yours the

moment I saw you sitting in that intersection. I couldn't stop thinking about you. I tried to draw you. I never thought I could even touch you. You're an angel on earth I would die to protect."

She could feel the tears welling up behind her eyes, from the flood of emotion that overcame her.

But she didn't have time for tears now.

She only had time for him, because she belonged to him, too.

She reached up and put her hands on his shoulders, the same way she had all those months ago. She didn't have to pull him down. He lifted her off her feet to kiss her.

"I am yours, too," she said against his lips. "*Raphael. Trey.*"

She let the names roll off her tongue. There was nothing strange about them. They were both him.

Stella kissed him, then, before she finally called him what she had really wanted to, all these years.

"*My angel.*"

ABOUT THE AUTHOR

Shirley Siaton writes edgy and evocative stories and poems. Her worlds are in a deliciously dark cross-section of the romance, neo-noir, action, fantasy, new adult, and contemporary genres.

She has several books of fiction and poetry released since February 2023. Her first book is the free verse collection *Black Cat and other poems*. She also pens juvenile literature as Shirley Parabia.

She is an award-winning writer, poet and journalist in English, Filipino and Hiligaynon, lauded by the Stevan Javellana Foundation, Philippine Information Agency, and West Visayas State University. Her essays, short stories, and poems have been published internationally in print and digital media. Her multi-lingual plays have been staged in the Philippines.

Shirley is a black belt in Shotokan Karate and an international certified fitness coach. Originally from Iloilo City, she is based in the Middle East with her husband and two daughters.

ON THE WEB

Shirley's official website:
shirleysiaton.com

Complete reading guide:
shirley.pub

Subscribe to Shirley's VIP list for free exclusive updates:
newsletter.shirleysiaton.com

www.ingramcontent.com/pod-product-compliance
Lightning Source LLC
LaVergne TN
LVHW040046080526
838202LV00045B/3508